TW(

C

———⚮———

PETER KENNEDY

Copyright © Peter Kennedy 2021
This book is sold subject to the condition that it shall not, by way of trade or otherwise, be lent, resold, hired out, or otherwise circulated without the publisher's prior consent in any form of binding or cover other than that in which it is published and without a similar condition including this condition being imposed on the subsequent publisher.
The moral right of Peter Kennedy has been asserted.
ISBN-13: 9798732748741

For Hans-Peter Hartung

This is a work of fiction. Names, characters, businesses, places, events and incidents are either the products of the author's imagination or used in a fictitious manner. Any resemblance to actual persons, living or dead, or actual events is purely coincidental.

ACKNOWLEDGEMENTS

This novel is the product of my own imagination. The episodes in the current time are drawn from my own experience as a medical doctor. The episodes based on the 18th century are also entirely imaginary and I have been informed and influenced in particular by the following books which I hereby acknowledge for their help and information. Any errors are entirely my own.

The magisterial book by Jerry White called *London In The 18th Century* 2012. The Bodley Head, London, in particular for the geography and housing of London.

The superlative biography by Wendy Moore of John Hunter called *The Knife Man* 2005. Bantam Press, Gt Britain, in particular for gaining insights into Hunter's character and appearance.

The extensive lexicon by Dean King called *The Sea Of Words* 1997, Henry Holt and Company, New York, in particular for the list of colloquial 18th century words.

The remarkable medical historical book by Ralph H Major called *Classic Descriptions Of Disease* 1965 3rd edition, Charles C Thomas, Illinois, USA, in particular for the classic disease timelines and original descriptions of a variety of diseases.

The extraordinarily fluent and exciting *Outlander* series of novels, especially number 5, *The Fiery Cross* by Diana Gabaldon, 2001, Penguin Random House, UK, in particular for their vivid reconstruction of 18th century customs and clothes.

I also thank Dr Catherine Kennedy for critical review of the manuscript.

CONTENTS

ACKNOWLEDGEMENTS i
CHAPTER 1 *A most thoughtful doctor of 2017* 1
CHAPTER 2 *A physician of his time in 1768* 9
CHAPTER 3 *A journal to remember* 19
CHAPTER 4 *A remarkably quick operation* 40
CHAPTER 5 *A difficult case even for 2017* 62
CHAPTER 6 *A difficult case especially for 1768* 77
CHAPTER 7 *The time for some welcome advice* 92
CHAPTER 8 *A most distinguished advisor* 109
CHAPTER 9 *A diagnosis is established* 129
CHAPTER 10 *No diagnosis is established* 137
CHAPTER 11 *History may or may not repeat itself* . 142
ABOUT THE AUTHOR 155

CHAPTER 1

A most thoughtful doctor of 2017

Dr Rupert Aston, a forty-two-year-old liberal and progressive medical consultant, is clever, conscientious and extremely inquisitive. Like many consultant neurologists, the so-called intellectuals of medicine, he has a longstanding and keen interest in medical history. An old consultant boss of his had told him a long time ago when he was still a humble medical student that a sound knowledge of the history of medicine was essential if a doctor was to truly understand the nature of illness and the patients' fears and expectation of what medicine can do for them. Though medical science and treatment had clearly advanced greatly over the previous hundred years, the bond between a patient and the doctor has probably changed very little from historical times, apart, of course from the modern approach in dealing with patients that ideally combines honesty, respect, compassion and empathy. Anyway, that's the general idea which everyone knows is not always realised in practice. Even in Rupert's parents' time a typical family doctor or hospital specialist had a definite tendency to talk down to their patients, and adopt a rather patronising and paternalistic stance. He even remembers that, just about. Perhaps that attitude, even more prevalent in previous centuries, was somehow necessary, or at least inevitable, given the rudimentary, if not primitive, state of medicine that existed even up to the beginning of the twentieth century. Yet from time immemorial there had always been a more cynical and realistic section of humanity that viewed most, if not all, doctors as greedy, and arrogant quacks who know little more about diseases than do their patients. Rupert reckons those cynics certainly had a point. Some of what was practised as good medicine in the past was truly horrific, and come to think of it, no more so than in the eighteenth century. What particularly appals Rupert is the near certainty and total confidence that these doctors of old had in relation to their often bizarre and profoundly ineffective treatments. But he himself is convinced that three great discoveries stand out like shining beacons that changed the whole practice of medicine and surgery. These he reckons have to be vaccinations against serious infections, anaesthetics and antibiotics. To live in a world without any of these terrifies him beyond measure. But what he doesn't yet realise is that he is one of the few people anywhere who truly can imagine life without these miracles of modern medicine. That is both his problem and his insight. That is not necessarily a contradiction.

*

He had just returned from a Tuesday morning outpatient session in which he saw five new neurological cases. He was due to see six but one patient didn't turn up with, as usual, no reason given. While the proper reaction to that should have been one of disappointment and appropriate annoyance, the truth is that he was quite relieved especially as it meant he could spend more time with the five who had bothered to attend, two of whom were particularly difficult and uncertain. So, he reminded himself, rather out of habit than anything else, the diagnostic tally that morning was two tension headaches that didn't need any brain scanning, a probable alcoholic peripheral neuropathy, a middle-aged man with possible early multiple system atrophy, and a woman with obvious Parkinson's disease but complicated by several other worrying neurological features that suggested to him that there was a lot more mischief going on in her nervous system than just one condition -the so-called Parkinson's disease plus. He had arranged for these last two patients to be admitted to one of the two neurological wards in the hospital for further assessment and investigation. He would almost certainly while she was an inpatient ask one of his closer colleagues with a specialist interest in movement disorders to see her to give his opinion. Clearly, allotting just thirty minutes each to a complicated neurological case was totally unrealistic if not downright dangerous. But in the present time of 2017 the clinical managers who hold most of the real hospital power these days apparently know rather better than highly trained and qualified specialists many of whom, like him, have multiple academic degrees. Rupert doesn't think it was always like this, and certainly not for his most senior colleagues in the profession. He is sure that some of the medical reforms over the previous two decades have certainly been good, but some have definitely made the working lives of medical doctors rather worse. The pendulum seems to have swung too far in one direction which may be better for the patients but not nearly so good for people like him. But he for sure would never want to regress to the dark old days of ignorance and inappropriate certainty of the medicine that was practised in past centuries. No, that would be a fate worse than death both for him, and, more importantly, for the poor trusting patients who indeed would sometimes literally succumb to the crazy or dangerous medical or surgical treatments rather than the undoubted perils of the disease. The reality is that most people just trust their doctors to do the best for them, and that has generally been the case since antiquity. And almost always, at least in the twenty-first century, that is certainly the case. Rupert may be a bit of a cynic but his heart is in the right place. And he's also an unusually insightful and instinctive medical doctor. Whether he knows that, however, is far less clear.

Rupert has been married for ten years to Jane, a laboratory technician at London University, and has two young children, a seven-year-old son called Peter and a five-year-old daughter named Alicia. By any current standards Rupert and Jane are happily married, and they each have great respect for the intellect and personal integrity of the other. That is something to be cherished, he thinks, as not all marriages are built on such a robust basis. A bonus is that they are both totally convinced that the other is very physically attractive. So they have what might be regarded as a full house in more than one sense.

*

Having finished his challenging morning clinic, Rupert strode along a long hospital corridor leading eventually to the stylish and somewhat dilapidated consultants' dining suite. Just as he entered the rather characterful and low ceilinged room he came across one of his most trusted medical colleagues, a specialist dermatologist who deals with diseases of the skin as opposed to the nervous system like him. He told Rupert all about one of his patients who has completely baffled him, and he thought he needed a talented and experienced neurologist to sort the problem out. Rupert was only too pleased to be of assistance and promised his friend that he would do his very best though it sounded like quite a challenge.

*

After a typically hurried and simple lunch, he briefly greeted a surgical colleague Mr Gerard Belmont-Smith, a patrician, very tall, and perfectly agreeable heart surgeon who was the current head of the hospital's distinguished, though historically troubled, Cardiothoracic unit. He had always liked this aristocratic and very well connected man whom he noticed was always impeccably dressed in the finest silk shirts and immaculate three-piece fitted suits made by Savile Row. The guy must be minted, Rupert told himself with little evidence of true envy or resentment. Still, he just could not resist ruminating on the generally greater prestige and political power and influence the top surgeons had both in his hospital and in general, so much so that he sometimes felt like a second-class citizen. And those surgeons who had a lucrative private practice were far richer than even a top rated physician could ever be. One only had to look at their cars, houses and, in some cases, boats in the sunny European resorts to see that was the case. Their income alone from carrying out private operations exceeds what he could ever hope to earn as a physician. This was not always true.

*

Later that evening, Rupert drove back to his comfortable house in West Hampstead, which is a pleasant and quite affluent middle-class area of London. As he entered the wooden front door of the house he noticed that there was a letter addressed to him and placed on the small hall table standing by itself just inside the hallway. He quickly opened the letter which was from his older brother Michael, a highly successful lawyer, saying that their recently departed father had left Rupert a box of old documents, some extremely old, about their recent and more ancient family. Apparently some of them appeared to be of considerable medical interest so he felt it only appropriate that he, Rupert, should take possession of them. The letters would be sent to him by the executors of their father's estate in a large case some time over the following two weeks. Rupert was intrigued and also expressed surprise and anticipation at what documents he might find. He knows from what he has been told by legions of aunts, uncles, great aunts and great uncles that he has several medical ancestors, some of them quite eminent in their local communities, especially in the eighteenth and nineteenth centuries. He wonders what gems of interest he might discover. The pleasure and excitement derived from the unknown should never be underestimated.

CHAPTER 2

A physician of his time in 1768

The year is 1768 and Dr William Aston is an experienced and already rather world-weary and cynical medical doctor with a particularly high professional and social status since he is a Physician rather than a Surgeon. The latter practitioners may have superior practical skills but it is the physicians who have the lion's share of the medical status as they are regarded as better and more rigorously educated and medically trained than their surgical counterparts.

The Royal College of Physicians carries with it far more prestige in medical and fashionable circles than does the Company of Surgeons which relatively recently in 1745 had split from what was previously called the Company of Barber-Surgeons. Social and intellectual snobbery is common to all the ages of man. He had obtained his academic qualification from no less than Edinburgh University which had produced many eminent medical practitioners. Although strictly speaking, only medical graduates of Oxford and Cambridge Universities were able to hold licenses to practice medicine in the district of London, in reality many other practitioners did so, including the apothecaries who, like most surgeons, did not possess a University medical degree. Furthermore, Edinburgh University graduates in Medicine were, on the whole, greatly respected in England's capital city and elsewhere in Europe. Born in the Westminster region of London city in 1730 to a fairly prosperous wine merchant, his family was always very comfortable without any significant want though by the standards of the time certainly not among the truly wealthy strata of London society. William was regarded by both himself and the rest of the population as already middle-aged at thirty-eight years. Both of his parents had recently died in their early sixties, his devoted mother of a galloping consumption and, in his gentle father's case, he was most cruelly struck down by a most severe and sudden fit of apoplexy. William was very fortunate to have survived the widespread perils of childhood as two of his sisters and one brother had all died in infancy, one from the measles, one from pneumonia with hydrops of the chest, and his older brother from the bloody flux. That only left William and his younger brother Thomas as living representatives of the Aston family. How William had managed to grow to a fine height of five feet nine inches - a good three or four inches taller than the average man of the times, though only about an inch or so taller than men in the American colonies - remains a mystery to him, especially since both his parents stood only slightly more than five feet.

*

William was also unusual compared with his fellow citizens over thirty years old in having almost all his own teeth still intact and still fairly healthily attached within his gums. He attributed this good fortune to his adoption of the modern advice from advanced French dentists who advise everyone to use a toothbrush every day. He brushed his teeth carefully twice a day without fail and also tried to eat as healthy a diet as possible. Being a prosperous individual in comparison to most of his London contemporaries, he could afford to buy a toothbrush, one with a silver handle in his case, and also eat a diet rich in fruit and vegetables with as little additional sugar as possible. He also had unusually white teeth since, unlike many people around at the time, he had never acquired the popular habit of tobacco smoking and chewing thereby sparing him a row of stained yellow teeth, assuming there is still a row of teeth to stain. While some of his medical colleagues still advertised the medicinal qualities of tobacco smoke, especially when directed up a patient's rectum, he never thought tobacco was a good thing for anyone. Many of his friends and colleagues regarded William as a bit of an eccentric because of this apparently healthy lifestyle, though a very clever one for sure, but he was the one with most of his teeth intact and who is, so far at least, mercifully free of bladder or kidney stones. What a remarkable manifestation of nature is mankind, he said to himself. He looked up at the sky and gave humble thanks to our fair and gentle Lord God for sparing him to look after the sick and unfortunate folk of the great city of London.

*

Of all things, bladder stones were very much on his mind this pleasantly bright morning in May 1768. He was not quite sure why this particular human affliction, quite awful as it is given its propensity to produce excruciating pain in the sufferer, should be so common in so many countries, and especially England, but he had a curious feeling that it may be something to do with people's diet. Maybe there's something about the food we eat or the different drinks we imbibe that makes us all so susceptible. He just doesn't know and neither does anyone else so far as he is aware. Famous figures throughout history such as Francis Bacon, Isaac Newton, Louis XIV, Oliver Cromwell and even his great hero William Harvey, discoverer of the circulation of the blood, suffered the scourge of bladder stones so perhaps they are just part of life and therefore inevitable. Indeed William, being a highly educated man, knows that the French philosopher and great humanist Michel de Montaigne, who also suffered from kidney stones, and considered himself to be old at the age of thirty-eight years of age, wrote somewhere that all men needed to be mentally prepared in life for the likely pain of stones. One of his more abstemious and religious colleagues suspects that these urinary stones are more common in people who drink too much red wine which also seems to predispose one to the affliction of gout but that's just a theory which may or may not contain some truth. The problem was that he just didn't know how to go about proving it.

Nevertheless he almost always tried to persuade his patients to be abstemious in their alcohol consumption whatever their particular fancy was, be it red wine, excessive beer, ale or gin.

Besides there were so many homeless drunkards roaming the streets of London, usually as filthy as the stinking ditches in which they were forced to live and sleep, that this was sound advice for anyone. Did not the great and recently deceased painter William Hogarth warn of the dangers of excessive consumption of wine and gin? The latter was a particularly severe societal problem at the time. Well at least it was clear to just about everyone that drinking dilute amounts of alcoholic beverages was a lot safer than drinking water which these days is a sure way of getting seriously poisoned. Only a madman, or else a person with a death wish, would stoop to such a thing.

*

He was that day travelling in London in an elegant post-chaise which had a dark black frame and a small but rather striking bespoke gilt emblem on both carriage doors, and was, quite unusually, sitting alone so he could stretch his body out to occupy a space that can normally accommodate two to three people, provided, of course, his fellow travellers were not too portly. He perceives that as being a trifle unlikely. He could have travelled in a more expensive licensed hackney coach, or even a Sedan Chair which would have been cheaper, but for some reason he felt uncomfortable about being carried around the streets of London by two fellow human beings however strong and fit they might be. It went against his life principles, and besides he had formed a sort of benign but rather one way friendship with Richard the coach driver to whom he wanted to give as much business as he could. William himself is as lean as a whippet and that is probably as much to do with good fortune - his parents were both slender people - as his careful, if not rather obsessional, eating habits. As his carriage makes its steady passage through the streets of London he becomes aware of the foul city smells of rotting sewage and much worse that waft their way into his carriage. He has over the years grown accustomed to this sad but repellent fact of London life and just for a moment imagines what living would be like without this daily insult to his olfactory system. But to do that is only to dream of Arcadian perfection and beauty and is completely unrealistic. But perhaps at some day in the distant future all that may change. But for now he must just endure such abominations which are just facts of life.

*

But William was travelling that morning with a specific purpose in mind. One of his long term patients, a distinguished and also extremely wealthy fifty-three-year-old man of business called Sir Joshua Turner, had a whole range of symptoms few of which caused William particular concern except for one. The poor man had suffered from increasingly severe pain in the pubic region, frequency of passing urine together with passing blood every time he took a 'piss' as it was so graphically explained to him. He also noticed that the pain was worse just as he finished passing water and had become truly agonising in its intensity. William, already renowned for his diagnostic acumen, confidently diagnosed the presence of bladder stone, a malady that was very frequent in the circles in which he practised. He had encouraged his patient to drink a great deal, within reason of course, in the hope that this might cause Sir Joshua to pass the stone or stones in his urine. But regrettably, despite consuming many pints of dilute ale, no stones were passed which left only one option as a last resort. So it was agreed that he would see a surgeon who was experienced in the very hazardous surgical procedure of lithotomy, or removal of urinary stones. The surgeon, a certain Mr John Aubrey, who was to carry out the operation, had only the previous week seen his patient who was willing to risk the pain and danger of the procedure just to rid himself of the daily suffering and humiliation which had made his everyday life almost unbearable for the previous year. Mr Aubrey, a rather kindly man of forty-three years, was already an experienced surgeon who had once as a young apprentice doctor seen the great British surgeon William Cheselden carry out a lithotomy on a patient in just one minute, and had now managed himself to master the tricky lithotomy technique as well as anyone in England though he was not quite as lightning fast as Cheselden. So, as far as William was concerned he was the best surgeon available in London, or for that matter anywhere, to do this particular operation and allow his patient to actually survive which was by no means certain. It was Mr Aubrey's personal residence near Hyde Park that his carriage was slowly transporting him to where the operation was to be performed in a specially designed and equipped room in the large and extremely elegant house where the surgeon carried out many of his operations, especially on his very important patients. He also had a permanent position as a staff surgeon at St George's Hospital, a leading London teaching hospital founded in 1733 where he had already established himself as a major surgical master, one with an unusually large private income from his noble trade. In William's opinion, Mr Aubrey was a true doctor and not, like so many of his arrogant surgical contemporaries, a butcher. The hospital was located in Lanesborough House in Hyde Park Corner not far from Mr Aubrey's personal residence, a close juxtaposition which was as useful as it is convenient. He was full of anticipation for what he was about to witness and was glad that the surgeon had invited him to witness the operation. That shows singular confidence to be sure.

CHAPTER 3

A journal to remember

After a busy day at the hospital Rupert is starting to relax in his home in West Hampstead, a comfortable four bedroom semi-detached house which was well positioned and elegantly furnished, but by no stretch of the imagination could it be described as a particularly affluent abode. It is a quality of house commensurate with his position in society and the associated regular, but not excessive, income from his permanent hospital post, supplemented only modestly by his weekly evening clinic in a centrally located private hospital. But in virtue of its prime location in London it would still sell for a good deal of money which would have bought a veritable mansion, if he and his wife Judith had so wished, in some provincial region of England or in most parts of Scotland and Wales. But he loved London for all its high expense and drawbacks and found the idea of relocating to another city inconceivable. That was a very common feeling amongst most of his friends and medical colleagues. There was something about London that was ingrained into his very being. Perhaps that was because of its rich history, its sheer diversity of every kind - cultural, professional, societal and architecturally - and the simple fact that it was the city where he had grown up and had always lived in apart from two productive years as a research trainee in his early thirties in America. This latter period was as exciting as it was also rather frightening but at the very least it had broadened his outlook and perspective on life. But London is his home.

*

He also enjoyed talking intimately with his wife Judith after a characteristically delicious supper of grilled salmon, sweet potatoes, asparagus and courgettes, followed by apple charlotte with ginger ice cream. A meal fit for a king he thinks to himself. The way to a man's heart may not be through his stomach, but for sure it certainly helps the general situation. His wife's exquisite cooking is something he truly recognises and values but it pales into insignificance compared to her other remarkable qualities such as kindness, compassion, insight, high intellect and, in his genuine opinion, physical beauty, a view shared by many of his otherwise critical colleagues. Her position as a biochemical laboratory technician is perfectly respectable, though not at all well paid, but it also belies the depth of her true intellectual powers which in his view are considerable. He knows he is a lucky man in more ways than one. From time to time he needs to remind himself of that fact. Soon after he is finished eating he spends twenty minutes practicing at the piano. There is a high quality upright piano in their main living room and he tries hard to spend at least a short period every evening developing his musical skills. That evening he decides to tackle one of the less technically difficult Mozart piano sonatas. He managed to get to Grade Eight with distinction on the piano in his last year at high school, but the real reason he plays is for pure enjoyment. Whether, however, those members of his family who listen to him practice derive quite as much pleasure as Rupert is an altogether different, and much less certain, issue. Though he is a fairly accomplished amateur pianist, he knows that his skill pales into complete insignificance compared with any of the professional concert pianists who grace our concert halls. The gulf is just too enormous, rather like the chasm that exists between an excellent club tennis player and the professional player whom one sees hitting the balls at Wimbledon. There is simply no comparison possible.

*

After he had finished practicing at the piano, and almost, but not quite, doing Mozart justice, Judith tells him that a large leather suitcase had arrived at their house by courier that very afternoon. She knows what it is, as does Rupert of course, and that it contains assorted papers and oddments bequeathed to him by his late father Dr James Aston. Before his mandatory retirement at the age of sixty-five yeas he had a thriving medical practice in North London.

He had recently died at the age of eighty-three years following a massive stroke. That had left his seventy-five-year-old mother Jane devastated and she would undoubtedly need a lot of support from both of her sons in the coming years. Judith had the battered looking brown suitcase placed in the spare room on the ground floor at the back of the house, a room that they used mainly to store small items of unwanted furniture and other whatnots or memorabilia they didn't have the heart to throw away. They are assuredly hoarders rather than discarders, but maybe he reckons that is not a bad thing to be guilty of. One never knows when an apparently useless item will suddenly become useful.

*

After helping Judith to put their two children to bed with as little fuss as possible, he decides to have a look at the papers his father had left him. He is too excited and impatient that evening to read them a story, something he thinks is hugely important and which he always greatly enjoys. Many different kinds of documents are contained within this large case which is old and battered with numerous small and large scratches and stains and it had clearly known better days. But it had survived the accumulated damage and physical insults. When William flicked open the rusty buckles and looked inside he was amazed at just how many folders, old medical reprints, ancient and more recent letters and family photographs were packed into the case. Some of the photographs were of his father's relatives in sepia images and a few were more recent pictures of his growing family showing William, his mother as a young woman and his older brother Michael, usually taken on their various family holidays in Italy and Spain. As he leafed through this treasure trove of documents his eyes were drawn to what was clearly a very old and tattered, time-damaged, heavily foxed, dark brown book which looked like some kind of journal. It smelled old and musty but he was intrigued by it all the same. There were no markings or titles on the hard cover of the book but when he opened it he saw that most of the first page had the following inscribed in faded but large black capital letters:

JOURNAL OF DR WILLIAM ASTON, PRACTISING PHYSICIAN OF LONDON DURING THE YEAR OF OUR LORD 1768 INCLUDING SOME REMARKS CONCERNING A MOST INTERESTING PATIENT

William had vaguely heard of this distant ancestor of his and he was very much aware that several of them had been medical doctors throughout the ensuing centuries. But none of them, so far as he was aware, ever became famous or even justified an entry in Wikipedia (though that didn't necessarily concern him in terms of their temporal importance). But he realised that such relative obscurity in no way precludes their high standing and influence during their own time. For all he knows this man may have been very important and highly regarded during his working lifetime in London. He just didn't know for sure, but assuming each generation lasts about thirty years or so, he reckoned this man may well have been nine generations back in his family line which would therefore make him his great-great-great-great-great-great-great grandfather. That was a lot of grandfathers! But though they share the same Aston surname they certainly would not have shared many of their genes. After all, he shared 50% of his genes with his father, 25% with his grandfather, 12% with his first cousins, so only a tiny part of his genome would be shared with this distant relative. But for certain they share an interest in medicine so in that way at least they have a kind of connection over nearly three centuries.

*

He then carefully turned the page and saw that it was indeed a personal journal that was entirely handwritten by its author. The handwriting was remarkable in that on first inspection it looked extremely neat and elegant, but his problem was that he had some difficulty in deciphering the individual words, a not uncommon problem when reading the writing of those in most strata of society in the eighteenth and nineteenth centuries. One of his biggest problems with reading old manuscripts was the use of the 'long s' which looks like an 'f' to modern readers, and this had always been an irritation for him. But fortunately the journal read fairly smoothly as William Aston did not use this 'f' form in his journal, and anyway the 'long s' began to fall out of favour in the second half of the eighteenth. Interestingly, he found that when he stood back a couple of feet from the text the words were easier to read.

This was a trick that his own loyal NHS secretary Joan had told him about since his own handwriting, like so many doctors, was so untidy and spidery that she found that the best, if not the only, way in which to decipher his medical hieroglyphics was to take a step back and try to read the whole line at a time so the overall pattern reveals the detail, as well as the context. It was a neat trick and he found that it worked very well with this ancient journal. He just needed to look at each sentence and paragraph as a whole and not in isolation. The pages were numbered and though they were yellow and old, with some of them looking rather moth eaten, nevertheless there were at least a hundred and twenty-two pages or so that he could read well and which might contain all kinds of detail and perhaps secrets. Rupert also wondered why his ancestor had bothered to keep a journal in the first place, and also why it was limited to just one year of his life. There was something odd about the whole thing and he was determined to get to the bottom of it, assuming of course that there was indeed something to find out. That was just an inspired hunch. Furthermore, if there wasn't anything strange to uncover then he was still extremely interested in this personal recollection in virtue of its relative antiquity and as a personal record of what it must have been like as a practising physician in former times. He also wondered whether his father had read William Aston's journal, and if he had, the question to answer is why he also wanted his son to read it. This was intriguing stuff.

*

Rupert was something of a polymath, just as his father had been, and had a wide knowledge of medicine, science, politics and philosophy both in the current time and also in the eighteenth and nineteenth centuries, with a very keen interest in the former. His almost legendary memory was also a great help. He picked up the journal, stepped out of the small spare room and walked the short distance on the same floor to his jam-packed study, a brightly lit room with perhaps two thousand books neatly arranged in many layers of fitted and not so fitted shelves. He sat down at his large mahogany desk, removed a few pieces of blank paper from its right upper drawer, picked up a dark blue biro pen from the desk surface and started to think and write down all the prominent eighteenth century figures he could think of. This was the sort of exercise that he rather enjoyed and reflected his somewhat obsessional nature.

*

He decided to write down as many famous names as he could in specific categories, though he realised his list could not possibly be a complete one. No-one is that well-informed. While composing this roll of honour, which he saw as an essential pre-requisite to reading his ancestor's journal, he was struck by how frequently scholars from Scotland figured which was remarkable for such a relatively small country. What a clever lot the Scots are, he thinks to himself.

*

Since he knew more about medicine and science than anything else, he decided to start with prominent figures in these two areas. Medical pioneers included Percival Potts (1714-1788) the founder of orthopaedic surgery, his student John Hunter (1728-1793), a surgeon and scientist who was probably the greatest medical figure of the eighteenth century who is rightly considered to be the father of scientific surgery, and Edward Jenner (1749-1823), who was John Hunter's apprentice, a physician who first developed a vaccine for small pox making him the founder of vaccination and immunology. Hunter would also have seen early in his medical career the great urological surgeon William Cheselden (1688-1752) operate with great speed and manual dexterity, and this century also included John Abernathy (1764-1831) an influential surgeon who was the founder of the great St Bartholomew's Hospital in St Pauls, London. Another innovative surgeon of that time who attempted ligation of large arteries was Astley Cooper (1768-1846).

*

He can think of so many scientists of this period that the long list truly amazes him when he creates it from memory. But where should he start? While the great Isaac Newton (1643-1726) did his groundbreaking work on gravitation, motion and optics in the second half of the seventeenth century, nevertheless his life did spill over to the eighteenth century. Likewise, the life of notable physician and collector Hans Sloane (1660-1753) also spanned both centuries but his life was even longer, especially for those perilous times. The shy and rather eccentric scientist Henry Cavendish (1731-1810) discovered hydrogen and determined the density of the Earth. No wonder the famous Cavendish laboratory in

Cambridge is named after him. The chemist Joseph Black (1728-1799) discovered magnesium, carbon dioxide and the nature of heat, and another great chemist, the scientist, polymath, theologian and philosopher Joseph Priestley (1733-1804), discovered several previously unknown gases, carbonated water and made major contributions to our knowledge of electricity. The great Michael Faraday (1791-1867), who discovered so much about electromagnetism and electrochemistry, was also born at the end of this century. The distinguished scientist John Dalton (1766-1844) was both a chemist and a physicist and proposed atomic theory, contributed greatly to meteorology, colour blindness and the laws of gases. He must also not forget the notable chemist Humphrey Davy (1778-1829) who discovered several elements using electrolysis and who invented the famous 'Davy Lamp.' And of course there was also the eminent French chemist Antoine Lavoisier (1743-1794), a scientific giant who discovered oxygen, explained the role of oxygen in combustion thereby debunking the then popular 'phlogiston' theory, put chemistry on a quantitative basis, and much more besides. What a terrible tragedy and loss to science it was when he was cruelly executed at the early age of fifty years on false charges by the bloodthirsty and murderous zealots of the French Revolution.

*

But William thinks he should not forget the inventors and explorers of this age. Captain James Cook (1728-1779) was a formidable naval officer, explorer and cartographer and enabled his scientific passenger Joseph Banks (1743-1820) to make major discoveries in science and botany. Banks went on to become a longstanding and influential President of the Royal Society. One of his heroes, Alexander Von Humboldt (1769-1859) was also a great explorer, scientist, writer on nature, and polymath. Then there was James Watt (1736-1819) the inventor of the steam engine which facilitated the onset of the industrial revolution.

*

The eighteenth century also included the working lives of several great philosophers. In his view the greatest of these, whose analysis of causality has never truly been refuted, was the outstanding empiricist David Hume (1711-1776). Like so many great thinkers he published his greatest work while still a young man - in his case in late twenties - which is truly remarkable. When he was older Hume became an historian and politician. Of all the philosophers he knows about, the one Rupert would most like to have met and dine with would be Hume, especially as he's sure he would have been charming and most interesting company. Frances Hutcheson (1694-1746) is perhaps less well known than some of the other philosophers but he was one of the founders of the Scottish Enlightenment, an early writer on the subject of aesthetics, and contributed significantly to important issues in ethics and moral philosophy. It is also significant that one of his pupils was no less than the philosopher Adam Smith (1723-1790) whose seminal and highly influential work 'The Wealth of Nations' was a precursor of the modern discipline of economics, and was also a key contributor to the Scottish Enlightenment. The French philosopher Montesquieu (1689-1755) was also highly influential in the fields of political philosophy and economics. While Jeremy Bentham (1748- 1832) is rightly regarded as the main proposer of the principle of Utilitarianism, Rupert does not entirely believe that such a world view is universally valid especially when some individuals use this principle to justify occasionally punishing the innocent to protect the majority. He recognises the historical importance of Bentham's ideas, and rather admires the man himself, but one must always pursue the ultimate reality to which a particular philosophical doctrine leads. He always links the great German philosopher Immanuel Kant (1724-1804) with Hume, especially as the latter was a large influence on the German thinker, but like so many people he finds that trying to read and understand Kant's works are a real challenge and some of them are downright obscure. So he rather prefers to read commentaries on and explanations of the writings themselves to original texts though he always tries to read both if he can. But Rupert certainly recognises the remarkably penetrating nature of Kant's world view. While he also appreciates the consistent and innate scepticism and immaterialism proposed by Bishop George Berkeley (1685-1753), and greatly admires the man's originality, he always finds that he just doesn't think his ideas are right.

But who is Rupert to judge such things?

*

Several influential writers also made their mark in the eighteenth century. Samuel Johnson, or Dr Johnson (1709-1784) as he is usually known, immediately comes to mind and books have been written about this literary giant of his times. His work as a literary critic, lexicographer, essayist, poet and much more place him in the very first rank of English literature, but as a neurologist Rupert is also very intrigued by Dr Johnson's reported tics and other mannerisms. He wonders about the true diagnosis. The satirical genius Jonathan Swift (1669-1745) saw right through the dishonesty and immorality of the government and society in which he lived, while Voltaire (1694-1778), an extraordinarily prolific polymath, was surely one of the greatest, if not the greatest literary figures of the eighteenth century admired by just about everyone including Rupert. Voltaire was a highly effective and articulate polemicist for sure, but he was so much more than that. Despite his criticism of religion, though, Rupert certainly does not like some of the anti-Semitic passages in his writings. No-one gets everything right, he thinks to himself. The eighteenth century also showcased the iconic poetry of the famous Scottish poet Robert Burns (1759-1796), the sublime and timeless romantic verse of William Wordsworth (1770-1859), the genius of his friend and contemporary poet Samuel Taylor Coleridge (1772-1834), and the extraordinary poems and engravings of William Blake (1757-1827). Another great poet of the age was the gifted Alexander Pope (1688-1744). Rupert thinks hard and recalls that this century also boasted the writers Daniel Defoe (1660-1731) and

Henry Fielding (1707-1754). The influential Scottish historical novelist Walter Scott (1771-1832) is another great literary figure of that time. Of course he must not forget two great German writers, J.W. von Goethe (1748-1832) the massively influential playwright, novelist, poet and polymath, and his great contemporary Friedrich Schiller (1759-1805) the playwright, philosopher, poet and polymath. Interestingly, Schiller also trained as a medical doctor.

*

His mind then turns toward music, and the extraordinary list impresses even himself. It was clearly a golden age of composers as almost all his favourite ones lived during that time. He is enormously impressed that the century boasted Ludwig van Beethoven (1770-1827), arguably the greatest composer who ever lived, Johann Sebastian Bach (1685-1750) and Wolfgang Amadeus Mozart (1756-1791). These three musical giants are probably the greatest composers of music of all time. He then realises that both George Frideric Handel (1685-1759), the composer of the sublime 'Messiah' no less, and Joseph Haydn (1732-1809) were also musical giants of this century, as was the prolific Venetian composer Antonio Vivaldi (1678-1741) and the equally prolific German composer Georg Philipp Telemann (1681-

1767). Both the legendary violinist and composer Nicolo Paganini (1782-1840) and the great violin maker Antonio Stradivari (1644-1737) also had lives that extended into the eighteenth century. Rupert did make a distinction between those whom he recognises as the greatest ever composers such as Beethoven, Bach and Mozart, and those who are his favourite composers such as the sublime Ralph Vaughn Williams in the contemporary period who, though still great, were not quite the same as these three colossal composers of the eighteenth century.

*

What about painters? This was less easy for him as this is not strictly one of his main interests. Nevertheless the list in his mind is still an extraordinary one. There were a wealth of fine painters of the time but to him the greatest was JMW Turner (1775-1851). If ever there was an artistic genius then it is assuredly Turner. His contemporary John Constable (1776-1837) was also a wonderful painter whose romantic landscape pictures fired Rupert's imagination. The portrait painter Joshua Reynolds (1723-1792) was also most impressive as was his rival, the portrait and landscape artist Thomas Gainsborough (1727-1788). One should not forget William Hogarth (1697-1764) who was not only a fine painter but also inculcated warnings and moral sentiments in some of his works. Another great portrait painter of that time was the very fashionable George Romney (1734-1802). In Europe he must not forget the brilliant romantic Spanish portrait painter and printmaker Francisco Goya (1746-1828), or Jacques-Louis David (1748-1828), the great French neoclassical painter.

*

Great politicians abound in the eighteenth century. Britain's first Prime Minister Robert Walpole (1676-1745) comes immediately to Rupert's mind, and two other of his distinguished successors in that high ranking role were William Pitt the Older, the first Earl of Chatham (1708-1776) and his relatively shorter lived but brilliant son William Pitt the Younger (1759-1806). The anti-slavery campaigner and consummate politician William Wilberforce (1759-1833) was a contemporary of the latter Prime Minister. The United States of America also had its fair share of highly gifted politicians. The founding fathers illustrate this well such as the modest and great first President of the US George Washington (1732-1799), the lawyer and second US President John Adams (1735-1826) and also two brilliant polymaths, namely the third US President Thomas Jefferson and main author of the historic Declaration of Independence (1743-1826) and Benjamin Franklin (1705-1790) who was not only a great politician and US founding father but also a legendary scientist who discovered so much about electricity and lightening.

*

At this point Rupert had almost exhausted his impressive knowledge of great figures who had lived in the 1700s, but not before he recalled several highly significant military commanders. These included the British naval hero Viscount Horatio Nelson (1758-1805), the highly successful soldier John Churchill, the first duke of Marlborough (1650-1722), and the military commander the Duke of Wellington (1769-1852) who was the eventual nemesis of the French military genius and dictator Napoleon Bonaparte (1769-1821).

*

This focussed and sustained act of recall has caused him just a little mental exhaustion, but after a few minutes he had regained his innate curiosity about his ancestor's journal. Then he had an unusual insight. It is quite remarkable that a century that contained such a wealth of blazing talent in all aspects of the Arts, and also to some extent in the physical sciences, should remain so utterly primitive in terms of its medical knowledge and practice. From his own knowledge of this time, which is certainly not inconsequential, he regards eighteenth century medicine as being dominated by ignorance, arrogance and quacks with the occasional enlightened pioneer. In particular, he can never quite understand the period's obsession with letting blood, usually using an instrument called a fleam or else with a lancet. While Rupert withdrew a patient's blood in order to examine its contents as a means of diagnosis, these primitive medical forerunners withdrew blood as a form of treatment especially for severe fevers. Thank goodness we have evolved since those times, he thinks to himself.

With these rather negative thoughts dominating his mind he then decides to start reading the historical journal. He decided to look at it both carefully and slowly, a few pages at a time. Perhaps he might even gain an insight or two. Somehow, he considered that most unlikely.

CHAPTER 4

A remarkably quick operation

After travelling for about thirty minutes across London in his carriage, the powerfully built coach driver slowly pulled back the reins of the two strong horses and stopped just a few yards away from Mr Aubrey's large and imposing house in Hyde Park Corner. William leaned out of the carriage door to catch the words addressed to him.

'I believe this is Mr Aubrey's house sir, and we have arrived five minutes early.'

'Thank you, Richard. You have done well. I am pleased and most grateful to you.'

'I thank you, sir.'

William felt a curious sense of anxiety about what he was about to witness for the first time. It was not that he was a particularly nervous or squeamish man, but he was very concerned with his having to witness the inevitable pain that his patient was certain to suffer. Laudanum can only do so much to ease the pain of the knife. He had actually been invited by Mr Aubrey to be present at the operation since it was he who had first referred him for the surgery. He always believed in continuity of care for his patients, unlike many of his medical brethren.

As he stepped out of the small coach William took a deep breath of the invigorating spring air and turned towards his driver.

'Richard, I should be obliged if you would collect me from this house in three hours' time.'

'As you wish you, sir,' was the polite and subtly obsequious reply.

*

As the coach sped off briskly along the long road in front of it, William took stock of the large, elegant house in front of him. Built in the neoclassical style and comprised mainly of blonde sandstone, his immediate impression was one of opulence. Though clearly struck with what he saw, nevertheless he was also somewhat sceptical about its origin as even a prominent surgeon of Mr Aubrey's high standing in the city would be most unlikely to earn a sufficient income from his practice alone to afford such a splendid abode. He wondered, just for a few seconds, whether he had inherited wealth or, even, perish the very thought, if he had had some other, possibly illegal, source of funds. Dismissing these negative and distinctly ungenerous thoughts, he looked around the extensive garden which was well kept and neat as he would have expected. In doing so he could not help noticing that there were at least twelve large windows in the front and both sides of the house. This was yet another indication of the surgeon's wealth because the government levied an unpopular window tax on any house owner whose abode contained seven or more windows - called by some 'daylight robbery'. Clearly this tax, though severely limiting in health, ventilation and also appearance, for most of London's poor citizens, was not any kind of inconvenience or problem for Mr Aubrey. In William's case, though his family was already quite prosperous, he had deliberately limited the number of what might pass for windows in his house to six because he was unwilling to pay this unpopular and unfair tax. He had even boarded up two windows in his house to avoid having to pay it. Mr Aubrey's entire double-fronted Georgian house, fashionably adorned by large masses of benignly spreading green ivy, and built on two floors, was surrounded on all sides by rows of many tall poplar and elder trees spread out in a geometrical pattern throughout the garden. Since it was a stunningly bright spring morning, the dappled sunlight streaming through the trees shone down in curious patterns across the front of the house, which faced in an easterly direction, as well as the rectangular paved courtyard region bridging the path to the main door which was large, blue, and graced by a golden knocker in its centre moulded in the form of a leopard. The overall effect was both pleasant and curiously hypnotic in its demonstration of soothing and natural beauty.

*

William seldom dons his best attire when going about his usual business, including seeing his patients when he generally dresses in hard wearing woollen garments, either in the private room in his house in Chiswick, or in the hospital where he is one of the few staff physicians. But on this occasion, which he felt was an important one, he wore his finest outfit which if he is honest with himself he rather enjoys. Clothes do indeed 'maketh the man'. So for this event he wears a white linen shirt with frilled cuffs at the end of long sleeves, a stylish yellow waistcoat adorned with gold embroidery at the sides, a spotless white stock across his neck, light brown breeches with white silk stockings and gold buckled shoes, and, even though it is spring, it is still somewhat on the chilly side, so he wears over these a narrow burgundy coloured justacorps coat. All his life he hated the wearing of wigs of any kind, even though many, if not most, of his distinguished contemporaries did so, and he despised the fine, scented powder used to adorn and perfume them even more. He could not even abide the smaller periwigs that gentlemen of the law usually wore in the various courts of justice. On rare public occasions, when he really had no choice in the matter, he was forced to don a wig, and the smallest one possible at that, but that was just the exception. Like many intellectuals of the time he liked to keep his hair long and he had a full head of luxurious jet black hair which was tied in a neat queue behind his head. The overall effect was quite fetching and there was no doubt that he was a dark and handsome fellow by any standards, something that his kind and dear wife Lizzie was frequently telling him. He was not at all sure of his good looks himself, being an intrinsically modest man with no traces of true vanity, but he was minded to believe everything that his wife tells him. And he certainly was not prepared to make an exception in this case.

*

He walked the few steps to the large door, pulled the gold knocker backwards and let it strike once. Within no more than a few seconds a pleasant faced young woman in her early twenties and wearing the simple clothes of a maidservant appeared and smiled at him politely.

'You are present sir for the operation?' she inquired.

'Yes indeed madam I am, though I fear I am slightly previous,' he replied.

'Not at all sir, I shall escort you to my master's special operating room directly.'

The young maid gave a slight but visible curtsey and led William into the house, first passing through a long hall adorned with a deep blue carpet, a low white patterned plaster ceiling and fine wooden panelling on either side. She then turned to the left and he had to walk through what was clearly one of the best and most elegant rooms of the house, one that was obviously designed and opulently furnished to entertain and impress, and not necessarily in that order.

While not exactly a large room, and while he only managed to experience its ambience and allure for just a few seconds as he walked through it, nevertheless that was enough to captivate him. The room, officially a drawing room, was circular in shape and adorned all round with elegant and very expensive walnut display cabinets and sideboards containing or supporting various small antique figurines and coloured plates of the highest quality. Sitting majestically on one of the larger sideboards was an exquisitely carved gold and white French mantel clock. The entire central floor area was covered with the latest and most fashionable Axminster carpet with a deep blue background interspersed with a rich multi-coloured floral design. The room's walls were decorated with the latest French design, green and white with an intricate pattern of birds and trees. A most beautiful square glass chandelier with multiple candle holders was suspended by a thick silver wire from the delicately carved ceiling, quite low and grey in colour. At one end below the single large window through which bright sunlight gently filtered was s small mahogany escritoire, and placed near the room's centre were two carved walnut sofas just next to which on either side were four highly decorative Italian armchairs to seat admiring visitors. Altogether it was a rich man's room that did everything it was meant to in terms of impressing its many guests.

Once out of the drawing room via one of its three

exit doors, all of which blended in with the walls so well that they were hardly visible as such, William was led by the maid through a narrow winding passage way. This was plain, being not at all embellished in any part, smelled vaguely of must, and soon revealed another door, a smaller one this time, through which he entered a large, relatively sparsely furnished but clearly specially equipped, high ceilinged room which functioned as the distinguished surgeon's home operating room. The floor was made of uncovered hardwood and the walls were simply decorated with plain grey wallpaper. One oval window at its far end allowed a small amount of sunlight to illuminate the room, but most of the lighting was necessary for what was carried out in it was provided by no less than six candle-holders spread out evenly towards the room's perimeter, each one of which was placed on low walnut sideboards and contained four beeswax candles which had yet to be lighted. The fact that the far more expensive and severely taxed beeswax rather than the much slower burning and relatively inexpensive tallow candles were being used here was itself testimony to Mr Aubrey's wealth. Perhaps he preferred, as might his unfortunate patients, the quite pleasant smell of melting beeswax to the more sickly smell of slow burning tallow, but the brief twenty minute burning life of the beeswax candles would be more than adequate for what was likely to be a surgical procedure lasting barely a few minutes or even less. Clearly, speed was the essence of the surgeon's success as well as his skill. In the centre of the room was a sight that William found rather sinister which was a clearly purpose built operating wooden table about six and a half feet in length and two feet wide. Below it was placed several large white sheets, presumably to catch and soak up the inevitable blood from the patient, and on the table's surface were placed two square shaped cream coloured pillows and two large white drapes for covering up the patient and more. Beside this table he could see a small low lying oak table upon which was placed numerous operating instruments including several sharp scalpels, two pairs of forceps-one small and the other quite large, a small saw, two metal probes and various other assorted implements. He could also discern several small bandages and what looked like many adhesive strips. This man clearly knows his trade. After all, as a practising surgeon he was probably someone's apprentice rather than a University graduate like him.

*

After just two minutes of waiting, the patient Sir

Joshua Turner arrived for his ordeal, flanked by two slim but very tall and strong looking young men dressed in ordinary woollen working clothes, one of whom was wearing a long coat and the other just a long jacket. The clearly anxious man was definitely unsteady on his feet and his eyelids were drooping intermittently, and he also had an obvious look of absolute terror even though he was gallantly trying to control his perfectly understandable fear. Soon afterwards a third man arrived, shorter, older and more heavily built, and he was carefully carrying a medium sized glass bottle containing a brownish red liquid which William was certain must be laudanum, that useful but also potentially addictive mixture of opium and alcohol. He reckoned that will help the patient only to a limited extent, and he had definitely been given a hefty dose already, even more necessary as Sir Joshua was a big man, in fact a rather unhealthy and overweight one who looked particularly vulnerable without his usual powdered wig and rich man's clothing. For this procedure he was only wearing a loosely fitting long white gown with nothing whatsoever underneath. The third man exchanged a few quiet words with the patient to whom he gave another laudanum drink from the glass he was also carrying.

Sir Joshua gave William a welcome look of recognition and smiled broadly at him. 'Good morning, Dr Aston, it is indeed very good to see you here.'

William gave him one of his typically pleasant and friendly smiles. 'Good morning to you, Sir Joshua.'

The patient was helped onto the wooden operating table by one of the younger men and looked anxiously towards William, saying a few words to him as he did so.

'Doctor Aston, a word with you sir, if you please.'

William walked quickly from the back of the room to Sir Joshua's side by the table. 'Before I submit myself to the surgeon's knife, can you please reassure me again of its absolute necessity?'

William put his hand gently on the clearly terrified man's shoulder and addressed him in a soft gentle voice.

'Sir, I can absolutely assure you this operation is of the utmost importance for your good health. We have tried every known medical remedy to rid you of the stone but alas nothing has worked. Surgery is our last resort but I can say to you unequivocally that this operation will have a most successful outcome…'

'Successful yes to be sure sir, but I have heard it

said that this procedure is most terribly painful, so much so that some people even die immediately or soon thereafter.'

William maintained his calm and reassuring demeanour.

'You must be aware Sir Joshua that your surgeon Mr John Aubrey is one of the finest operators in London and is vastly experienced in what we doctors call a lithotomy which as you are aware means removal of a bladder stone. His speed of operating is truly astonishing and while this will inevitably cause you a surfeit of pain, I can assure you that it will be brief, a few minutes at most. Then you will be rid forever of the terrible pain of the stone. Let me assure you sir that you are in the finest hands available. Besides the pain of the knife will most surely be much lessened by the laudanum drug you have been given.'

Sir Joshua's worried expression relaxed just a little on hearing this.

'Thank you for your assurance Doctor Aston. Indeed this is what I had heard about Mr Aubrey. But…' At this point the poor man seemed lost for words or perhaps fear had made him lose his train of thought.

'Yes, you were going to say…?'

'Will I survive? Will I be alright afterwards and witness another dawn?'

'Many, many more dawns for certain. I have every confidence of that.'

'I thank you sir,' was the sadly forlorn reply. 'I know I must be a man and be brave.'

At this point the surgeon himself briskly entered the operating room together with a nervous but intelligent looking young man, presumably his apprentice and who immediately lit all the beeswax candles in the room. Mr Aubrey himself was rather short and stout, had an open, friendly and rather pleasant face, was wearing a long white apron which William noted was heavily encrusted with a plethora of dried blood, and was carrying another glass container which he was sure must contain yet more laudanum. He also had, almost in contrast to the rest of his body, a pair of elegant hands with long delicate fingers. That observation itself made William relax a little though he was quite sure the patient had failed to notice them. The surgeon acknowledged with a smile and a wave William's presence near the back of the room to where he had just moved, and quickly greeted his patient by smiling broadly and reassuringly as he shook his hand.

'Well met sir, this won't take very long at all. Are you ready?'

Sir Joshua pursed his lips as if to embolden himself for the upcoming ordeal and spoke a few nervous words.

'Thank you Mr Aubrey. I suppose I am as ready as I shall ever be, the Lord help me.'

Mr Aubrey puts his arm around his patient's shoulders to steady his nerves and reassure him. He perceives that the man is exceptionally anxious, as would be any normal and intelligent person.

'Here have one last draught of laudanum. It will calm your nerves and dull the pain.'

Sir Joshua manages to drink a little of the rather bitter liquid and then lies back on the pillow, resigned to the agony that he knows he is about to experience.

'Well, Sir Joshua,' the surgeon says to him, 'we should feel rather honoured as your splendid physician is here too to witness the proceedings.'

'Yes that is most kind, as are you sir. I do feel honoured in that sense at least.'

'Now my assistants will hold you firmly and keep you steady while I get rid of this stone for you. The whole procedure should take no longer than two or three minutes or so.'

'My word sir that is quick work indeed.'

'Quite so, quite so,' was the reply but Mr Aubrey's attention was already elsewhere and was getting down to the regrettable but necessary task before him.

*

The two young men took a firm but gentle hold on each leg on either side and pulled the patient's legs backwards into the classical lithotomy position, undignified for certain but the only possible position in this case. Then the older man, clearly the strongest, placed a thick leather strap in Sir Joshua's mouth to stop him biting his tongue off from the pain, and placed both his hands on the poor man's shoulders and held him in a firm vice-like embrace to prevent any unnecessary movement. However much the patient might move and squirm in agony, no effort on his part could ever break that iron grip, both powerful and benign in equal measure.

*

Mr Aubrey did not waste any time on preliminaries. He gave a quick knowing glance to the older man, picked up one of the scalpels beside him and commenced the operation. With his left bare hand he identified the perineal region between the man's scrotum and anus and made a deep incision just to the right side of this point. Immediately, dark red blood poured freely from the wound which his young apprentice quickly staunched with a thick linen bandage. Clearly he had assisted at this kind of procedure before. As the first knife cut was made the patient winced and screwed up his eyes, but when Mr Aubrey cut deeper into his sensitive flesh the pain had clearly become almost unbearable. William was impressed with the sheer speed and manual dexterity of the surgeon who also seemed to have a total mastery of the local anatomy. Perhaps that was not surprising since, like many surgeons before him, he had been a lecturer in anatomy at his hospital for several years prior to dissecting real people.

*

As Mr Aubrey manipulated his forceps into the bladder he could see that Sir Joshua was in indescribably severe pain and distress, despite having been heavily dosed with laudanum. William saw that though the patient's automatic attempts to move his body were completely limited by the three powerful assistants, nevertheless he was now making rhythmic muffled screaming noises, quite terrible to witness. In a curious way, these manifestations of terrible pain were even worse to see than a full throated and ungagged bellowing. William felt slightly nauseated, not by the sight of blood to which he had long been accustomed, but by the sight of such hideous suffering. He even felt a gripping sensation in his bowels. But after exactly two minutes and forty-seven seconds, as measured by William's pocket watch which he had removed from its snug position in a waistcoat pocket, the operation was over as Mr Aubrey had managed to extract two stones from the bladder. That was remarkably quick work, though not quite as quick as the great William Cheselden might have taken. Both stones were whitish-grey, one was quite large and the other small, both visible to all present when the blood had been removed from them with a cloth by his assistant who was now pushing a large, thick white linen bandage against the operation wound. The leather gag was removed from Sir Joshua who had tears of agony and relief streaming down his face. While he was unable to prevent himself from quietly sobbing, both from the pain endured, and, indeed to a lesser extent still ongoing, and also a measure of gratitude, William could also discern a measure of relief on his flushed pink face.

Mr Aubrey placed the two stones in a round metal dish and showed them somewhat proudly to his patient who was now in less pain and breathing deeply.

'Give you joy of your courage sir and for being finally rid of the stone,' said Mr Aubrey.

'I thank you sir for your attention. But the pain was even worse than I might ever have imagined.'

The surgeon looked at him kindly and placed his right hand, still bloody from the procedure, on the right shoulder of his patient before reassuring him further.

'Sir Joshua, I feel compelled to tell you that you are one of the bravest patients I have ever operated upon. Indeed, my word you were wondrously brave. I am full of the most exceptional admiration for how you have endured the sadly very necessary and inevitable discomfort and pain of the knife.'

'I think pain rather than just discomfort will answer most aptly,' replied Sir Joshua, 'but I thank you sir all the same.'

'Quite so, quite so,' added Mr Aubrey.

At this the surgeon made a brief signal to his three assistants, all of whom remained impassive, yet slightly sweating, following which they gently lifted the patient and carried him away to rest and recuperate in another room in the large house. But just before they did that, they gave him a further drink from the bottle of laudanum.

William then moved away from the back of the room and began a conversation with Mr Aubrey.

'Mr Aubrey, I congratulate you sir. That was truly a most remarkable display of the surgeon's skill. You removed his stones in just under three minutes.'

'Is that correct? That is longer than I had thought. I had hoped for just two minutes.... Hmm. Anyway, they are out now and I am hopeful for a full recovery.'

'How likely do you consider that is?' asked William.

'Well,' replied the surgeon, 'to be sure he has had a major shock to his system but he did not drop dead during the operation, which I am afraid sometimes happens, and as far as I can see so far there is unlikely to be a surfeit of blood loss. Besides, any blood loss may do him a little good.'

William rather doubts that is very likely but keeps his own counsel and says nothing.

'I shall keep him here in my house for about two days where I shall arrange for two of my maid servants to care for him while he heals physically and in his mind. Then he can go back home to Richmond where his wife can look after him. I am expecting to speak with her later today.'

'That is very good.'

Mr Aubrey then looked more serious.

'Mark you, William, there is still the serious danger of wound suppuration. We have packed it with clean bandages but in the event that a germ infection develops, especially if it then led to blood poisoning then the outlook will be very poor indeed.'

'But how likely is that sir?'

'I think, God willing, that he may recover well without complications. His wound will be dressed twice daily and he is after all a very fit gentleman though he is rather elderly and I believe is rather too fond of the proverbial drink.'

'Indeed he is both of those,' adds William, 'but if I may be permitted to enquire of you, how many of the patients who undergo this operation actually survive?'

Mr Aubrey smiled benignly at this and answered the question directly.

'Well, to be candid, I have performed this procedure on precisely forty occasions and to date twenty-seven patients have survived. Of the thirteen who did not, five died from shock on the operating table, two died from unstoppable blood loss and six died from wound suppuration and blood poisoning.'

'So, as I calculate it, about two thirds of your

patients survive the operation. I must congratulate you sir on a remarkably successful outcome, one entirely due to your skill.'

'I thank you. Speed is of the essence you will understand. A slow and delayed operation just will not answer.' He washed his bloody hands in a porcelain bowl of warm clean water as he says this.

'Yes, I can well understand that,' adds William.

'William there are just two other matters I want to ask you.'

'Why of course, I will do whatever I can.'

Mr Aubrey's face relaxed slightly and he spoke further.

'First I should be both obliged and honoured if you would dine with me for luncheon here in my home. Cook has made some particularly agreeable meat dishes for our enjoyment.'

'I should be more than delighted to join you. Thank you most kindly, sir.'

'The other favour is rather less straightforward. I know how skilled you are in diagnostics.'

'I try my best....'

'Oh come, come, William, no modesty please. I know how good you are. Everyone knows that. Look,

I have a most difficult and complex case under my care on the ward in the hospital. I am quite certain that his complaints are medical rather than surgical, but to be candid I have little or no idea what the blazes is the matter with him. I think he requires the careful attentions of a physician. So I immediately thought that you were the man.'

'That is very kind of you. I shall be delighted to assist in any way I can.'

'Splendid,' said Mr Aubrey, gently patting William on the back. 'I can tell you all about him over lunch. I don't know about you, but after all this activity I am quite clemmed.'

CHAPTER 5

A difficult case even for 2017

Rupert sighed deeply and closed the historic journal, not greatly surprised at the events recounted there, but all the same as a twenty-first century physician he was still pretty appalled. It was not so much the lack of sterility and antisepsis that upset him, but more the notion that these two eighteenth century doctors, both clearly at the top of their respective professions, really thought that a 33% mortality rate for a surgical procedure was a good outcome. In his view, by his own modern standards, such a failure rate would be unthinkable and probably criminal, and anything more than a 5% mortality rate would be totally unacceptable for any surgical procedure, and even that rate would need to be a worst case analysis. How times change, he thinks to himself.

What really strikes him about the eighteenth century is the remarkable discrepancy between its groundbreaking achievements in music, literature, philosophy, painting and science on the one hand and the almost total lack of progress in clinical medicine and surgery on the other.

The great discoveries in vaccination, anaesthetics and antibiotics had to wait until the nineteenth and twentieth centuries to become part of everyday existence. Probably their single most significant problem was the near total ignorance about the root causes of disease - indeed the doctors and scientists of that time did not even know about the existence and disease-causing role of bacteria and viruses so they were flying somewhat blind so to speak. Their theories about the different causes of diseases were also bizarre and just plain wrong.

The notion that many diseases were due to imbalances in the four main 'humors', namely black bile, yellow bile, phlegm and blood - an ancient Greek belief - and that treatment should aim to restore the normal balance of these in sick patents struck Rupert as being utterly simplistic if not downright imbecilic. As far as he could see eighteenth century medical treatment for all human diseases relied heavily on just a few ludicrous remedies. So they could make a person vomit using emetics or give people purgatives, both of these designed to rid the patient of unwanted harmful fluids or other matter thereby restoring a normal bodily balance of the humors. They would also use a fleam or else a lancet to bleed the patient of many ounces of blood as a form of therapy which had no logical basis at all and often did more harm than any good. Or they might calm nerves or dull the misery of acute or persistent pain or other untreatable chronic conditions using opium, usually in the form of laudanum which was a concoction of alcohol and opium. Other ridiculous remedies included Peruvian bark for all fevers (whereas the quinine component of bark would only be effective in the fever due to malaria) or even inappropriate use of very toxic 'medicines' containing arsenic and mercury for certain chronic conditions. Usually all those doctors were capable of doing was to reassure their poor, trusting patients, and maybe relieve some of their more troublesome symptoms with such soothing unguents as Lucatellus's balsam or various poultices to relieve inflammation. They might also administer a range of 'tonics' most, if not all, of which were utterly useless. Any perceived benefit of their unscientific remedies was almost certainly due to the age old 'placebo effect'. Of course, with their various plant-derived remedies, they might occasionally get lucky if the extract also happened to contain a truly effective drug as in the case of foxglove which consists of the powerful heart drug digitalis. It seemed to Rupert that, frankly, these doctors really didn't have a clue about most diseases. He recalls the eminent twentieth century philosopher and mathematician Bertrand Russell once saying when specifically asked that if he had to live in another time period he would choose to be an eighteenth century French aristocrat (before the revolution of course). Rupert totally disagrees as at that time in history there would have been a total absence of proper dentists, local or general anaesthetics, vaccinations, antibiotics, antisepsis, antenatal or perinatal care, surgical know-how, knowledge of basic microbiology or anti-cancer drugs or radiotherapy. If you were very healthy and never had any significant illness throughout life then there were certainly agreeable aspects to be alive in such an elegant age provided you were wealthy and well connected, of course, but in practice such a rosy scenario was most unrealistic. While fascinated by the past, he was more than happy to live in the present.

*

With these rather negative thoughts in mind, Rupert realised the hour was getting late. Reading and thinking deeply was more tiring than he might have realised, and he eventually climbed under his bed covers and went to sleep, wrapped closely within the gentle arms of a semi-comatose Judith, all the while hoping that the horror of what he had just read would not induce nightmares. He had an unfortunate tendency to experience night terrors on a regular basis as he was so impressionable. During the daytime he was an entirely rational being. But at night things were very different. At such times he was subject to a plethora of nocturnal irrationality. He was certainly not alone in that.

*

That Wednesday morning Rupert had an unusual sense of urgency and felt like a man in a hurry. His medical colleague and friend had asked him to see what had proved to be a 'difficult case' which, just like the description of a patient being 'interesting', invariably means something quite different to him. What those terms actually signify is that so far no-one actually had a clue as to what was wrong with the unfortunate patient, and that his doctors were pretty desperate to get help. Either that is true, or they feel completely out of their depth, or, perhaps more likely, the reality is a combination of both. But whatever the expectations of him or the inconvenience, as this was meant to be his one and only research day of the week, Rupert always liked a challenge and he had a powerful and idealistic sense of duty. That is probably why he is where he is in his profession.

*

He arrived early that day in the hospital's massive indoor car park, making sure that he deposited his grey automatic Audi in the bespoke third level staff floor, and made his way up through two austere stone staircases into the main corridor of the sprawling hospital. After walking briskly through several wooden swing doors, two more indoor flights of stairs and a final long and impersonal green coloured corridor, he arrived at the deceptively modern medical ward 2 to see and give his expert opinion on the man himself, a certain Mr Henry McNeil Grayson. This man's curious medical condition had so far baffled a host of clever doctors, though he had yet to be seen by a specialist neurologist. One of the patient's more junior doctors had strongly indicated to Rupert that he thought the patient's problems were very possibly due to psychological causes, often euphemistically referred to as a 'functional' disorder. That immediately put him on his guard since, in his experience, patients labelled as 'functional' frequently turned out to have a true organic disease underlying their symptoms and signs. Never give medical labels to anyone.

*

As Rupert entered the ward he felt an odd *frisson* of anxiety which was most unusual for him, and the reason for this escaped him. He hoped too much was not expected of him, though he knew he was extremely astute in patient diagnosis, and, far more important, he also possessed that somewhat intangible quality of *flair* that allowed him to see things that others did not. If that was really the case then he truly had no idea where such ability came from. What he did know, however, is that it had been noticed by his superiors very early on his career, even as far back as medical school. Surely they can't all have been wrong about that?

*

With his customary politeness he made himself known to the ward sister in charge, a friendly middle-aged woman with an open kindly face who greeted and thanked him warmly for coming. After the usual pleasantries he spent about ten minutes looking carefully through the patient's medical notes which were already extensive and thick. The sister then escorted him to a discrete side ward on the far left of the symmetrically rectangular ward complex where Mr Grayson was sitting up in bed listening to the radio through a pair of large earphones. As they entered the room the man gave him a pleasant smile and spoke to him in a soft lisping voice.

'Doctor Aston, I presume.'

'Yes,' replied Rupert, 'right first time. I'm already impressed.'

At this, Henry laughed out loud and extended his hand which Rupert immediately and warmly took in his and shook it firmly but gently. This was a good start.

'So they've asked you to sort out my problem then?'

'I'll certainly do my best to do that,' Rupert replied in earnest.

'Well I wish you the best of British luck with that. I believe I'm a bit of a mystery.' Henry smiled ruefully as he said this.

In less than thirty seconds, Rupert's trained and expert eye took in and assessed the man in front of him. Henry Grayson was fifty-three years old but looked at least ten years older. He was thin and pale, and his weather beaten face was fixed in an almost permanent frown that belied the intrinsically humorous and puckish nature of his true personality. His facial skin was covered with small unhealthy looking black spots some of which looked distinctly suspicious, but Rupert was no dermatologist. The man's eyes were small in size, light blue in colour and bloodshot, with just a slight degree of rheum that would periodically pour from them onto his slightly sunken cheeks. He had a small amount of stubble, most marked on his small chin, which presumably reflected either inattention to his daily ablutions or else perhaps an innate sensitivity of his skin. His nose was straight and narrow, almost Roman in its nobility, which made it his best feature and rather out of place with the rest of his face. He had a thick head of grey greasy hair with a widow's peak at the front, and a wide mouth which he tended to keep closed when he smiled, perhaps in an attempt to hide the many rotting or absent front teeth which probably reflected a lifetime of dental neglect or else poor nourishment, or, more likely still, both. Yet as a teenager his dentition had clearly been good as evidenced by the many intact and filling-filled teeth in the rest of his mouth. But whatever else Henry may show, or chose to show, to other people, his face told the acute observer that he had at least had a life, though perhaps not one that was full of much joy. Overall, Rupert thought, this man was never really healthy as an adult, but for sure at that moment he was definitely unwell, and any notion of his being 'functional' was entirely mistaken. This much the experienced physician knew just by looking at his patient.

*

Having made the customary introductions and passed the necessary phase of pleasantries, Rupert got down seriously to the business in hand. He generally found that a detailed and meticulous history from the patient was likely to reveal the diagnosis in most cases, and if he hadn't worked out what was going on after that, then he was unlikely to arrive at a correct diagnosis from the subsequent examination stage. In such a scenario, which he suspected was going to be the case here, ultimate success would depend on further consideration, with or without some discussion and advice from colleagues, and a raft of detailed investigations. If necessary he would have no hesitation whatsoever in getting help from other doctors as he had not the slightest degree of arrogance. But that may also reflect a slight lack of self-belief. Whatever the reason for this, it made him a particularly careful and conscientious doctor.

*

After about forty minutes of direct questioning, which he tried hard to make as comfortable and relaxed as possible, Rupert had gained a great deal of information about Henry.

Unfortunately, his initial feeling was correct in that he still had little, or at least very little, idea of what was actually the matter with him. But there was one thing he knew for certain. Whatever the underlying diagnosis might be, assuming of course that there was just one cause of the entire clinical picture, it was definitely real, 'organic' rather than 'functional', and almost certainly serious. Rupert has always been a 'lumper' rather than a 'splitter' and he always looked for the one root cause of the patient's problem. But he also had an open mind, and it was imperative to think widely.

*

This much Rupert had gleaned from his benign interrogation. Henry McNeil Grayson was born in Bournemouth in the South Coast of England where his parents were both teachers in the local primary school. His middle name, which he hardly ever used, might indicate a Scottish influence in his family tree decades, if not many generations in the past. He had a fairly good education as a teenager but did not attend

University. He had a large number of jobs but by the far the longest was as an able seaman in the Merchant Navy where he spent fifteen years of his life until ten years before, and where he also developed a taste both for the wonders of the sea and the taste of fish rather than meat. In this post he had travelled widely and had visited many cities in five continents and had once worked briefly in a West African gold mine. Before this he had worked as a labourer for a construction company, an auxiliary nurse in his city's main hospital, as a salesman in a London shoe shop, and an assistant in a funeral business. But since his discharge from the navy he had been continuously unemployed despite trying hard to find useful employment. He was receiving unemployment benefit and lived alone in a one bedroom council flat in East London. He had never married, both his parents had died, his father of a massive stroke and his mother of ovarian cancer, and he had one brother whom he hadn't seen for about eight years. Rupert found the whole life story rather sad, but Henry was not in the least bit sorry for himself, and he did appear to enjoy life to some extent, particularly when he had access to malt whisky which he said he only drank in moderation. Rupert rather doubted that. Not surprisingly, however, he smoked twenty cigarettes a day, and had done so for as long as he could remember. Henry did not have much of a social life, but enjoyed watching television and film DVDs in his one bedroom council flat, and was also a member of what sounded to Rupert like some kind of religious movement, or sect, but he rather doubted whether that had any relevance to his clinical problems.

*

His current symptoms had started about eight months before. While he had never felt entirely healthy, he slowly became aware of an insidious deterioration in his general health and knew instinctively that all was not well. His arms and legs, usually very strong after many years of manual labour, not to mention the physical rigours of a short lifetime at sea, started to feel slightly weaker than normal making walking and performing hand movements such as writing or opening jam jars rather difficult. He also had a slight lack of feeling in his limbs but this did not worry him nearly so much. His appetite was normal and there had been no significant weight loss. That was really all that he'd noticed himself apart from perhaps a greater than usual tendency to be irritable and get upset at even small things which was unusual for him as his natural temper was an even one. What had really worried him was what was said to him by other people, especially some of the more outspoken members of his club, or sect or whatever it was. Rupert would find out about these people later and might even manage to talk with them. Apparently, so they had told Henry, he sometimes got his words mixed up making it difficult to understand what he was saying to them, and on occasion he had appeared not to hear what was being said to him. They had also noticed that his personality had changed somewhat in that he was quicker than normal to anger and sometimes seemed to get upset more easily than before . Henry himself had been unaware of some, but not all, of this but he simply relayed this second-hand information to Rupert. So far as he knew, no-one in his family had ever complained of any similar symptoms.

*

When Rupert examined him he did not find very much, if anything, that could help him in hisdiagnosis. Apart from his generally rather unhealthy state, all he'd managed to detect during a detailed physical examination was possibly a very fine tremor of the outstretched hands (which could be related to a high alcohol intake he reckons or else a benign sort of tremor), and he had rather brisk tendon reflexes which was completely against a diagnosis of a peripheral neuropathy - that is a loss of function of the nerves in the arms and legs.

Henry gave a very good account of himself and apart from perhaps a little slowing up of his answers to the many questions, he showed no obvious evidence of a developing dementia. In any case, clearly the man required a detailed and extensive set of investigations, and Rupert made a long entry in the notes in his well-nigh indecipherable handwriting, and recommended a large number of tests that he thought might help them reach a diagnosis.

Some investigations had, of course, already been done such as some routine blood tests, a chest X-ray and a CT brain scan but all of these had been normal, which was not in the least bit a surprise to him. Clearly much further thought and delving, as well as further more discerning and sensitive tests, would be required to unlock the secrets of Mr Henry Grayson's curious illness.

CHAPTER 6

A difficult case especially for 1768

After a sumptuous lunch with a rather elated Mr Aubrey, William was thinking hard about his life and profession as he returned in the small but comfortable carriage to his house in Chiswick. Though just outside the city of London, Chiswick, officially located within the region of Middlesex, was easily reached by carriage from the main city centre and it was sufficiently near yet also far away for William to escape the filth, stink and ever present dangers of inner city life within the nation's capital. Though he never met him in person, William was also rather proud that one of his artistic heroes, the great painter William Hogarth, had a splendid residence in Chiswick, and not that far from his home. Hogarth had died only four years previously and was a great philanthropist as well as an artist of great talent and importance. Another man he greatly admired, the late poet Alexander Pope, also lived in Chiswick in the early part of the century which also made him feel that he was living in an artistically distinguished area.

*

Yet William was increasingly convinced that the medical profession did not do a great deal for the average person. Somehow he knew that the physician's practice was very limited to just a few basic remedies and these seldom did the patient much good. But while he had such an insight into these shortcomings, he was just not able or original enough to make the breakthrough that he just knew must come one day. So he expressed little about his doubts and concerns to his colleagues who, if they truly knew what he thought, would possibly ostracise him as an unsafe doctor. As for the surgeons, they could certainly cure certain conditions, as he had only that day witnessed, but surely one day such operations might be performed without the terrible pain of the knife. Perhaps one day, which may be tens or even hundreds of years in the future, such a more humane way of treating peoples' diseases might be achieved. But it certainly wouldn't be accomplished by him. He may be an intelligent medical cove but for certain he was not a genius.

*

He eventually arrived at his own house, a large double fronted grey stone built residence that he had inherited from his father, and which boasted no less than six bedrooms, a discreet outside privy, a small but elegant drawing room containing a wooden spinet of which he was rather proud, a large kitchen with a small scullery and pantry adjoining it, a larger dining room and a small study for his own use, one that was adorned with numerous shelves on which he had packed a vast array of books on many subjects other than medicine. It was a fine house to be sure, and one with a neat expansive garden at the back which displayed a beautiful array of multi-coloured flowers on both sides as well as both an apple and a pear tree which only produced fruit every other year. He knew well enough that he was more than lucky to own it, something good that had happened to him purely through fortunate providence. Notwithstanding his material gain and relative wealth, he still greatly missed his loving parents. When one door closes then another one opens, as the saying goes, he thought to himself. With every passing day of his life he was acutely aware of how very true that saying was.

*

By seven o'clock in the evening William, his wife Lizzie and their two young children, seven- year- old Charles and five-year-old Anne, had all finished their evening meal. After Lizzie had put the children to bed having read a popular but rather frightening children's story to them for twenty minutes, she sat in their cosy drawing room in her favourite armchair in sympathetic conversation with her husband who appeared curiously agitated after the day's minor adventure. Lizzie was the love of his life and in truth he was most dreadfully fearful of losing her to one of the scores of fatal diseases that were so prevalent at the time, especially as she was such a wonderful mother to their two children. He was he was only too aware that life was a precarious gift that could be taken away from any of his family in the breadth of a day or two. As a physician he was more aware of this sad fact of life than most of the population. What was unusual was his curious discomfort at this awareness rather than the almost universal acceptance of life's fragility that most people of his time just took for granted. He wondered whether this would always be the case.

*

William and Lizzie spoke to each other softly and intimately as they sat facing each other in adjacent armchairs close to the open hearth in front of the flickering log fire. They absorbed the gentle heat radiating from the warming fire that slowly burned with intermittent shafts of dappled light and sparks that seemed to jump from wood to air. Though it was already May, nevertheless the evening was cool, and the cold stone floor that withdrew much of the heat from the atmosphere did little to raise the ambient temperature or make them feel more comfortable. He confessed to her his feelings of inadequacy and how little he thought doctors such as he actually did for their patients. Lizzie reassured him that he was doing the very best he could, and through her perceptive and sensitive arguments, tactfully but still forcefully expressed, William found to his surprise that he was greatly comforted by his wife. Unusually for the time, he listened carefully to his wife for whom he had the highest personal regard and utmost respect. Lizzie, wearing a simple long cream-coloured gown, and whose fine head of auburn hair was concealed beneath a white linen flat cap almost completely covering her delicate head, was also a rather fine musician and around nine o'clock she decided to play a little for him on the wooden spinet that dominated much of the small room in which they had intimately spoken to each other. She rose to make herself comfortable on the low stool by the instrument and began to play from memory, softly and carefully. William immediately recognised the composer, Johan Sebastian Bach, but was unsure about the piece. As Lizzie played for both of them, he closed his eyes and let his consciousness float effortlessly along the sublime music, one of Bach's many keyboard pieces originally written for the pianoforte, with its exquisite undulation of counterpoint and fugue. While letting the exquisite harmonies somehow cleanse his soul, he had absolutely no doubt that one day in the future this composer would become greatly revered and perhaps even worshipped as a musical genius. Yes, he had no doubt about that whatsoever.

*

The man's name was Abraham Atkins, and Mr Aubrey was clearly way out of his depth. In fact William had no idea why the patient's family doctor had referred him to a surgeon in the first place. Be that as it may, he had been given a task to do and he had every intention of doing it well and as thoroughly as possible. Regrettably these two goals are not always exactly the same though in his idealistic view they certainly should be. The original surgical referral could certainly not have been for significant financial gain as Mr Atkins was not a rich man, in fact quite the contrary. He wondered whether Mr Aubrey had a sense of charity in which case he had rather misjudged the man, and unfairly at that.

*

Individuals such as Abraham would normally be seen by a physician or apothecary in his own home, and for a fee, but unusually in this case Mr Aubrey had arranged for a consultation by William on one of the rather dreary ward cubicles in his own hospital. St George's Hospital was still quite recently developed as an Institution for treating the sick, but it had very quickly established an impressive reputation in London where it was still one of the very few major teaching hospitals in the city. During his brief hospital stay Abraham was being cared for very well by his sister Alice who seemed to be devoted to him and brought him regular meals and changed his linen every day.

*

Just one day after witnessing Mr Aubrey's lithotomy operation nearby, William prepared himself with paper, pen and his fine brain and experience to see his new patient. After his coach driver Richard had deposited him at the large iron hospital gates, he walked briskly into the main hospital where a uniformed porter, holding a long quill pen and sitting on a high chair and desk recognised and greeted him politely and with great respect. As he eventually entered the claustrophobic cubicle which housed a rather basic and very uncomfortable looking mattress which was laying on the ground with a few old and musty blankets and a dirty white sheet, Abraham Atkins and his younger sister immediately stood up and smiled obsequiously at the well dressed and distinguished young doctor who greeted them formally but politely.

'Mr Abraham Atkins, I presume?' enquired William, knowingly.

'At your service sir, you must be the distinguished physician Dr William Aston.' William felt slightly uncomfortable at hearing this but was nevertheless impassive and professional.

'I am Dr Aston, and I am pleased to make your acquaintance.'

'Thank you sir, I am delighted to make yours. May I please introduce my sister Alice.'

William smiled at this and raised his right hand in complete acquiescence. 'It is a pleasure madam. I see you are taking good care of your brother.'

Alice, a very thin woman aged about thirty-nine years despite her looking much older with a mass of untidy curly grey hair, gave William a polite curtsey and looked down at the floor rather than straight at him.

'I am honoured sir to meet you and that you are present to treat my brother Abraham... he has suffered greatly as I am sure he will recount to you.'

William felt an immediate rush of compassion for them both and spoke to her kindly.

'Yes indeed that is why Mr Aubrey asked me to see him... but please both of you please do sit you down on these two chairs just over there.'

Just after he said this William quickly moved two simple wooden chairs from the back of the cubicle to a point next to the mattress so they were both seated. Following this considerate act he sat down on the rather more comfortable upholstered chair that had been left there specifically for his use.

After all three of them sat down, William made a quick visual assessment of his patient before starting to ask him a series of penetrating questions. He had no objection at all to Alice being present throughout the history taking though that would not be allowed when the time came to examine her brother.

*

Abraham Atkins was a wiry forty-eight-year-old man but looked considerably older due to a combination of his remarkably weather beaten face covered with old pock marks, and his stooped posture despite standing almost six feet tall when he was made to stand up straight. He had thinning grey-black hair which grew curly at the sides and had a large bulbous nose below a pair of remarkably bright brown eyes which exerted a penetrating gaze that seemed somehow out of place with the rest of his face which was characteristic of a much older man. He had a wide thin mouth and surprisingly good teeth, so far as could be seen, especially so when his rather poor background and diet were taken into consideration, not to mention his apparent history of scurvy. While hardly a picture of good health, he did not strike William as a particularly ill-looking man, but he revised this initial opinion after hearing about his symptoms which concerned him greatly.

*

He managed to find out quite a few details about Abraham's life and symptoms. He was born in the town of Weymouth in Dorset, one of five children, three of whom had died from various causes in infancy. Since that time he and his only surviving younger sister Alice had remained very close. His family moved to London when he was twelve years old where his father managed to establish a moderately successful hat making business. Abraham attended school until the age of thirteen when he became apprenticed to his father and within a few years he had become a very efficient hatter-indeed the felt hats that were so popular at the time became his specialty. When he was eighteen he became bored as a hatter and sought freedom and adventure. He joined the marines, and was easily accepted in view of his tall, powerful frame and eagerness to serve his country. After two years of service in various cities in England he unexpectedly found himself recruited to Commodore George Anson's epic sea voyage around the world in 1740. He had been a marine stationed on the *Centurion*, the squadron's flagship, and after many adventures, acquisition of prizes, sea battles and gross hardships, he somehow survived and was one of the fortunate ten per cent of the original almost two thousand souls who had originally set out on the voyage from Spithead. During this time he had suffered from a large number of maladies including the inevitable and widespread scurvy which caused his gums to bleed and some of his teeth to become somewhat loose, as well as a disabling lassitude. But for reasons which escape him these distressing symptoms almost disappeared after he had been given fruit, mainly oranges, to eat soon after their ship had taken on fresh provisions near South America. William also did not understand this and remained sceptical, thinking this might well have been just a coincidence. When Abraham eventually returned to England at the end of the long voyage, he spent a further fifteen years as a marine, serving in the Royal Navy. William was impressed that at no stage in their conversation did Abraham express anything other than the highest regard for the Commodore who had led the squadron. That spoke well of both Abraham and George Anson. While his everyday life was generally a hard one, nevertheless Abraham was a strong man and he managed to see a great deal of the world. Not surprisingly he also managed to pick up a dose of venereal disease along the way during his naval career but this was by no means unusual, and in some respects almost inevitable.

*

He eventually left the navy at the age of thirty-nine years, and for the next nine years until the present time he had taken on a large number of different jobs. The most recent was that of a porter in Billingsgate fish market which was not very well paid and barely allowed him to pay the rent on the modest lodgings in

Whitechapel that he shared with his younger sister Alice. While Alice had remained a spinster, Abraham had been briefly married to a younger twenty-three-year-old and very sweet natured woman called Barbara. But tragically, after just one year of marriage she had died in childbirth and Abraham was forced to have the baby boy adopted by a wealthy doctor and his wife. Fortunately, Alice earned more than her older brother in her post as a maidservant to a wealthy lawyer's family who lived in the fashionable region of Hanover Square, and her wages, though still relatively meagre, were sufficient to keep the heartless bailiffs at bay and also food on the table to keep them both alive and in reasonably good health. It was a hard, if not joyless, existence for them both, but at least they had survived.

*

His symptoms had started about six months previously. They started insidiously and he became aware of an abnormal feeling in his arms, and, to a lesser extent, in his legs. During his work as a porter in the fish market he had increasing difficulty in carrying heavy loads which was essential in his work. His hands tended to shake slightly, even when he wasn't trying to use them, and also felt generally tired, even more so than would be normal after a hard day's manual work. His sister had also noticed that he was more irritable than before though he had always been a man who was quick to take offence and show anger. He had also joined what his sister thought was some kind of religious sect and had regular weekly meetings with his fellow members, or brethren, or whatever they call themselves. Abraham had mentioned to her that some of these people had told him to hold his temper rather better than he did, while others had expressed some concern about his obvious mood changes which they had noticed with increasing alarm. He told her he was afraid he might even be expelled from the only social life he enjoyed. Abraham himself, however, had little knowledge or insight into how his general mood had changed.

*

All that William had heard caused him a good deal of worry, not the least because he had almost no idea what was ailing the poor man. He then went on to give his patient a quick and rather cursory examination, and apart from slightly tremulous hands and a rather unreliable memory for past events and dates, he truly could not detect anything that would be regarded as sinister. But he knew very well that this could not conceal something very serious lurking throughout the man's body. His medical instinct told him that Abraham was not a well man.

*

But what could he do for him with his limited abilities to heal anyone? Both Mr Aubrey and Mr Atkins, along with his devoted sister, would certainly expect him to do something. But the question was what? William would certainly not bleed him just to be seen to be active, as it would benefit the patient very little, and probably not at all. He would, however, most definitely advise a thorough examination of the patient's urine in an attempt to gain some clues. He did, out of a combination of expectation and necessity, give Abraham a rather bitter 'tonic' which would certainly not do him any harm despite having no chance whatsoever of doing him any good. No, he was most certain that he needed help, indeed a second opinion. He thought for a while before smiling to himself. He knew exactly whose advice he should seek - a fine, visionary doctor who practised his art and experimented just a few minutes away from him in the same hospital. It was a requisite time to pen a short letter to the great man.

CHAPTER 7

The time for some welcome advice

Rupert was a bright physician for sure, but he was also aware of his own limitations and knew that he should seek help when it was the right thing to do for the benefit of the patient. He was completely bereft of arrogance or inappropriate self-assurance. As he sat in his comfortable upholstered chair in his small but cosy hospital office quietly contemplating a range of issues, not least of which was the nature of Henry Grayson's illness, he made an important choice. He would discuss the case with his slightly senior colleague, Dr John Rapello, a superb consultant in the large Neurology department, one who had the widest differential diagnosis of anyone he knew for just about any condition that was presented to him. John was originally of Italian descent and was not only a brilliant neurologist - in Rupert's opinion probably the finest in London if not the country - but also a most charming and helpful man. He was also deeply compassionate. Indeed he was, as they say, the *'go to'* doctor for one's family, friends or just about anyone, especially if the problem was a complex one. John Rapello was also a man easily prone to laughter, and with his distinctive machine gun crackling type laugh which might break out at any opportune moment, one always knew when he was nearby. His presence also had the unusual effect of making just about everyone in his benign vicinity feel better than they actually did, and that for certain is a rare gift.

*

When he eventually managed to meet up with John Rapello in the latter's equally small hospital office located in the outpatient department, he found him to be extremely attentive, listening carefully to every word Rupert said to him. It was interesting that there appeared to be almost an inverse relationship between the ability and standing of the medical doctor and the size of his or her private office. Though Rupert felt somewhat flattered if that really was the case, he also felt a distinct sense of outrage that so many physicians and surgeons in the hospital were clearly under the administrative thumbs of the managers some of whom he either tolerated or actively disliked. Notwithstanding this, the two careful doctors went over Mr Grayson's entire history as well as the few definite examination findings, and at various points in the narrative John politely interrupted him in order to clarify some important point or other. But of course, what may appear on the surface to be a feature of minor importance could easily prove to be something critical, and this was his senior colleague's particular strength.

*

When Rupert had finished his account of his patient, John smiled broadly showing his fine set of even white teeth, thought for a few seconds, placed both hands on his lap and began to speak and give his assessment.

'So Rupert,' he said, 'essentially we have an early middle-aged man with a progressive personality and memory deterioration together with a bit of tremor and some soft signs. Do I have that right?'

'Yes that's just about it in a nutshell.'

'All of his investigations you tell me are normal or anyway don't show anything to worry about. That includes a normal CT brain scan, MRI scan of the brain and cervical spine, chest X-ray, EEG, electrodiagnostic (EMG) studies of his limbs, cerebrospinal fluid (CSF), and numerous blood tests.'

Rupert concurs. 'Yes that's right. All these have come back normal.'

John then frowns and suddenly looks more serious as he thrusts his head towards Rupert. 'So can you tell me Rupert why Mr Grayson doesn't have Creutzfeldt-Jakob disease (CJD)?' This took Rupert rather by surprise though this possibility had occurred to him.

'Well,' he replied, 'the normal brain imaging, normal EEG (assuming it is not the new variant of CJD), and CSF are all against it.'

'That's true enough but we need more detailed investigation for this.'

'Such as…?'

John went on. 'Well I presume the MRI scan of the brain did not have a thalamic pulvinar sign diagnostic of CJD?'

'That's correct, John.'

'Yes but I suggest you repeat the scan using specialist FLAIR imaging and specifically ask the neuroradiologists to look for it. It's a long shot of course but still worth doing. Also, I suggest you repeat the CSF examination and ask some fancy lab to look for the 14-3-3 protein.'

'But that isn't specific for CJD is it?'

'That's perfectly true but it may give us another clue if it comes back as positive. Also, I am concerned about the normal EMG. As you know in CJD you can occasionally get evidence of a lower motor neuron problem even if the hand wasting and muscle fasciculation is not obviously evident clinically. The normal routine nerve conduction studies don't exclude it so this needs to be repeated raising this specific issue.'

'Indeed,' agreed Rupert.

'And I forgot to ask you. What did the formal psychometric report say?'

'We have asked for that of course, but it hasn't been done yet.'

'Fair enough,' said John, 'it might give us more information.'

'I'll let you know the results of these as soon as they become available.'

'Thanks Rupert. Of course it almost certainly isn't CJD but it would be awful to miss it. Actually I rather wonder whether this isn't some form of other neurodegeneration. There are now so many of these around, and as you know the more we do advanced genetics on our neurological patients then the more of these rare neurodegenerations we identify.'

Rupert smiled ruefully at this.

'Yes I have noticed that. I personally find it rather confusing.'

John shows his teeth again and said, 'But we have neurogenetic clinics to deal with that.'

'True enough. What I can also tell you is that he doesn't have any evidence of orthostatic hypotension - his blood pressure doesn't drop into his boots when he stands up.'

'Good to hear that. That was going to be my next suggestion. Rupert you have well and truly pre-empted me.' At this John gives his machine gun laugh which lasted nearly fifteen seconds. 'But there are two other things that I suggest you do.'

'Only two,' says Rupert half joking.

'Yes. Your patient sounds just a little unusual and I just wonder whether he hasn't been self-medicating or taking something inadvertently.'

'That's a good point. I very much doubt it but I guess either of those is possible.' 'Yes so I think you need to do an extensive toxicology screen And I mean look for everything - drugs, heavy metals, poisons, the lot.'

Rupert looked alarmed for the first time during their conversation.

'You mention poisons, John. But who on earth would want to poison the poor man?'

'You never know the intricate details of other peoples' lives. I am always surprised when I hear the secrets people have in their private lives, and I mean people who on the surface seem to be completely normal or even rather boring. It could all be a cover for something sinister.'

'But how would you know that if no-one owned up, which they certainly wouldn't?'

'Well,' John went on, 'sometimes in deliberate poisoning cases the patient improves markedly while in hospital for prolonged periods, only to then deteriorate when they go back home. The cycle then gets repeated. But don't worry that's only a remote possibility with your man. I'm almost sorry now that I mentioned it.'

'Well I'm rather glad you did. The thought hadn't even crossed my mind.'

John became suddenly more serious again.

'There is one other thing that I suggest you do. I

don't like the sounds of this sect, religious group or whatever it is. You mentioned that these people, whoever they are, provide some kind of social life for him. I guess he must be pretty lonely in that little flat of his especially if he hadn't managed to get a job for these last nine years. Why don't you ask him whether he could give you a name or two of people that he knows in this sect? Then you can meet them in person and make your own judgement. They may even give you some extra and very valuable information about how he's been these last few months.'

Rupert looked a little surprised but agreed to do what his colleague suggested. 'You know I'm not a detective John, private or otherwise.'

'Rupert all good doctors are in reality detectives of the body.'

'Just call me Sherlock Aston.'

'Rupert Aston sounds just fine to me.'

*

Henry Grayson saw no problem at all in telling Rupert more about his social club. As far as Rupert could understand, the club members did not comprise any kind of religious sect. Quite the contrary, if anything it sounded to him as if religion or indeed a belief in any kind of all - powerful deity didn't even come into it. He told Rupert that they were just very good people who wanted to help a fellow human being in trouble. This group of individuals seemed more likely to be akin to an unusual, if not maverick, kind of social worker who specialised in supporting such unfortunate and lonely people as Henry whom no doubt they perceived as lame ducks. But they were clearly a different type of grouping than regular social workers or other kinds of community welfare worker. These people had no regulatory body that defined their remit or behaviour, and Rupert had a nagging suspicion that they had some ulterior motive for their apparently selfless and benign support for the down and out. Surely, he thought, they must have some kind of underlying belief or motivation that makes them do what they do. Yet there are a few people around who are just plain good just as there are other folk on our landscape who are just plain bad. Maybe these people are in that first category, and he has seen enough of the world to know that there are those who just have a curious affinity with the weak and vulnerable. While Henry was weak, and getting weaker all the time, by no stretch of the imagination could he be regarded as vulnerable. He had to find out more about their motives. But the key issue was their possible relevance to his illness.

Rupert had arranged to meet with two members of the 'club', or whatever it was, in central London in a coffee shop within easy access from the local subway. After exiting Leicester Square underground station he walked the short distance along the narrow street past The National Portrait Gallery on his right and then into Trafalgar Square with the imposing façade of the National Gallery at one end, and also the commanding sight of Nelson's Column arising like a giant mast from the impressive square. He then turned left into the correct street according to the clear directions given to him and then finally he saw the small coffee shop with a green front on the right side of the road. He entered the rather plain entrance and immediately noticed two people, a young man and an equally young woman sitting at a table at the far end of the shop. They also recognised him instantly and they both stood up to greet him as he approached their table.

*

The man was probably in his late twenties, was dressed casually in blue jeans and an open necked, short-sleeved shirt, had closely cropped black hair, and both his arms showed extensive tattoos though it was difficult to see precisely what these showed. He had quite an intense look about him. The woman looked a similar age, was quite attractive in his view, had auburn hair held in place by a brown plastic hairband, wore a long blue dress with a red floral pattern on the front, and also a small metal ring that pierced and penetrated her right nostril.

She also had a similarly intense expression though she smiled at him rather more than did her colleague.

'You must be Dr Aston, Henry's doctor,' said the young man who introduced himself as Nick.

"Yes indeed,' replied Rupert, 'and it's a real pleasure to meet you both. Thank you so much for coming to meet me.'

'It's a pleasure for us too doctor. By the way, it is Rupert isn't it? ' Rupert smiled at them both and nodded his head.

'And this is Samantha.' As he introduced the young woman to Rupert, she smiled at him sweetly.

'And it's a real pleasure to meet you,' he said politely to Samantha.

'You too, doctor.'

'So,' Rupert said, 'let me get us all some drinks. What will you have?'

'That's very kind of you,' said Nick, 'I'll have an espresso if I may…'

'And thanks, Rupert, I'll have a cappuccino,' she added.

'I'll have a cappuccino too,' added Rupert.

After he'd ordered the coffees he lost no time in getting down to the business in hand. 'So,' he started, 'I'd be very interested in your organisation and how you've been helping poor old Henry Grayson.' He knew Henry wasn't exactly old but the phrase seemed right. Nick spoke first, and as he did so Samantha fixed her gaze on Rupert, but not in an intimidating way. Both of them had a particular way of speaking in which almost every sentence had its pitch raised at the end making it sound like a question - so-called 'upspeak'.

They also had the remarkable facility of never sounding a 't' sound in any word during their conversation. Rupert wondered whether these speech patterns were just copied from their fashionable contemporaries or else merely came naturally. He was mildly amused at this but not concerned, except that it made him wonder whether he was getting just a little old.

'Well Rupert, first off, we are not actually an organisation. We are basically a group of about ten people, mainly young in their late twenties or early thirties, but two of us are really old in their fifties, who have a strong social conscience…'

'Very strong,' interjected Samantha as she touched her nose ring lightly.

'Yes we have very strong convictions. None of us has any powerful religious affiliations or beliefs, so we are definitely not a religious sect, just in case you'd heard indirectly that we were and especially if you were worried about that.'

'Perish the very thought,' replied Rupert, trying to suppress a smile that may have been misinterpreted, 'so how exactly would you describe yourselves?'

Nick thought for a moment before responding.

'We are like-minded people who all live very near each other in West London - Chiswick as it happens - and we sort of like to catch people who are in need of help but who've been let down by the welfare system.'

'Well there's certainly no shortage of them, that's for sure,' said Rupert.

'Indeed there isn't and we got together to try as a group to help poor people like Henry Grayson who find themselves down on their luck and helped very little by the system.'

'The system?' asked Rupert.

'Yes the system, all of it, government support,

welfare, inadequate income support, food banks - in fact the whole pathetic lot...'

'Pathetic,' added Samantha.

'Exactly right, absolutely pathetic, so we try to help people. That's all we do.'

At this point of the conversation, which Rupert thought was just a little surreal, a serving assistant brought their three coffees to the table. All of them were accompanied by a small plain Italian biscuit which, in Samantha's case, she immediately gave to Nick in a way that suggested they were intimately acquainted. Rupert wondered whether Nick and Samantha were partners in life or whether theirs was an entirely friendly but professional relationship. But either way, it had little relevance to what they were discussing. He still rather suspected they were boy and girlfriend.

As they started to drink their coffees, which he noticed were excellent for once, Rupert asked the question that had been on his mind for a very long time.

'But what I'm not quite clear about Nick is how you identify these poor souls in the first place.'

'That's an entirely legitimate question,' replied Nick.

'Absolutely legitimate,' added Samantha.

Nick went on.

'The short answer is by word of mouth.'

'Word of mouth?' asked Rupert, rather surprised at this simple answer.

'Yes,' confirmed Nick, 'we find out about deserving people largely through information we get informally from friends and acquaintances. We have a lot of contacts you see.'

'So people don't contact you as is the case for The Samaritans.'

'Absolutely not,' replied Samantha, and as she said this Rupert noticed that Nick was nodding vigorously.

'Right, I see,' added Rupert, not seeing clearly at all, but he held his tongue.

'You see,' said Nick rather proudly, 'we find out about these people who have been treated badly by the system and who are falling into an abyss, and we befriend them and give them all the support we can…'

'Does that include financial support?' asked Rupert.

'Sometimes it does, but actually not usually. We generally try to support these people more in the emotional sense. We visit them in their homes and include them in our outings and social activities and that sort of thing.'

'I see, very good,' said Rupert who was beginning to understand these people a little more. 'And then of course as you know poor Henry got ill, or at least we think he's ill though we're not entirely sure that he does. He tends to deny a lot of things.'

'Indeed he does,' agreed Rupert.

'Anyway, whatever is the matter with Henry, even if it's something relatively trivial and not serious at all, he will have all our total support.'

'That's good to hear,' said Rupert.

There was then quite an uncomfortable pause in the conversation for about fifteen seconds until Nick asked his key question.

'By the way Rupert can you please tell us what you think is actually the matter with Henry? Does he have a serious medical condition?'

'Why? Do you think he has?' asked Rupert quizzically.

'Well, we're not clever doctors like you. But we don't think he looks at all well though he seems to be eating normally. And, how he just loves his fish meals.'

'Really? And what sort of fish does he normally eat?'

Nick and Samantha looked at each other but only Nick replied.

'Henry loves seafood, any kind he can his teeth into, but especially swordfish and tuna when he can lay his hands on them as they're pretty expensive these days. I guess that must be a legacy of his merchant navy days at sea. It's also a real pity he didn't make any profit from working in that African gold mine all those years ago. '

'I guess so,' replied Rupert, 'you may be right about that.'

They continued talking about all kinds of things after this, but none of them had any direct relevance to Henry. They all got on pretty well considering they had only just met. Either that or they were all being very polite.

*

Eventually, after a meeting lasting nearly an hour, Rupert thanked them both for their time, got up from the table and left the café, but not before Nick and Samantha had thanked him warmly both for giving up his own valuable time and for the coffees. Rupert's overriding impression of them was that they were completely harmless do-gooders even though they were somewhat eccentric, and perhaps just a little misguided. But whatever Henry's illness was, these people had nothing to do with it.

CHAPTER 8

A most distinguished advisor

William could not help feeing a distinct *frisson* of excitement, not to mention anxiety, at the prospect of meeting one of the country's most brilliant and extraordinary surgeons. John Hunter may have been only two years older than he, but he was already recognised as a medical scientist of the highest order and was also a fellow of the Royal Society, a remarkable early recognition of his scientific achievements. Like William, he was also on the staff at St George's Hospital though employed as a surgeon rather than a physician. That appointment had been made only recently, and they had never actually met, something that William thought distinctly remiss of him. He had sent the brilliant surgeon a long and detailed letter about Abraham Atkins in the hope and also expectation that he would be able to give him some sound advice as to his patient's true diagnosis. But for this meeting the arrangement was for them to meet at Mr Hunter's own home, a large house in Jermyn Street which had previously been the abode of his older brother William who had gained an outstanding reputation in anatomy. Interestingly, he had met the suave William Hunter in person as an anatomy teacher but not his younger brother. He was somewhat relieved, if truth were to be told, that their meeting venue was not to be John Hunter's other residence in Earl's Court where he owned a house and extensive farmlands which housed a large array of different animals and where a great deal of pioneering animal experimentation was carried out. William did not feel that such an environment would be most conducive to the type of discussion he sought with the great man.

*

William arrived at the surgeon's London house in the early afternoon of a dull early June day. He gave instructions to his coach driver Richard to return to the residence after two hours, and then made his way, somewhat nervously, to the main front door on which he knocked gently. After a short interval he was greeted politely by an elderly lady, whom he thought was probably an important or senior house servant based on her unusually authoritative manner and comparatively smart uniform, who led him through a long hall which led at its end to her master's study. As soon as he entered the room he saw John Hunter himself who immediately stood up from his desk, smiled politely, though perhaps not very warmly, and introduced himself with more courtesy than he had expected.

'It is a pleasure to meet you at last Aston,' said Hunter.

'The pleasure and honour is mine,' William replied bowing his head slightly, 'your servant sir.'

Over the course of just a few seconds William took in the surgeon's general appearance and manner. He stood a good six inches shorter than William and, by contrast, was quite stout in build, but this did not detract from his general demeanour which was one of a most distinguished nature. He was not wearing a wig, and wore his hair quite long, and this alone made William warm to him as this was evidence that he was not a member of the elite social establishment though of course intellectually he was at the ultra-elite level. The surgeon wore a long brown jacket, a yellow waistcoat over a simple white shirt and conventional light brown breeches. He had an unusually intense and intelligent pair of eyes which seemed to be as focussed to the same extent as his concentration. Yet he also had a rather strange and perhaps unexpected look about him as if he was thinking about something completely different to what the observer might perceive was the case. So he had the mental capacity to be both highly focussed on a problem while also taking a broader and original view. That is a capital combination. After spending just five minutes in his presence and engaging in conversation with him, William was in no doubt whatsoever that he was in the presence of a visionary and innovative genius.

*

Hunter did not waste time in uttering pleasantries and got down to the matter in hand withoutdelay.

'Well, William, I have looked through your detailed letter to me about this man, and there are a few questions I would like to ask you, if that is agreeable to you?'

'Yes of course, Mr Hunter,' William replied, 'please ask whatever you wish.'

The surgeon gazed at the physician with an intensity and seriousness of purpose that William found daunting and reassuring in equal measure.

'First of all, do you know the exact duration of his

symptoms? Do you think it at all possible that he may have been suffering these infirmities for much longer than he reports to you?'

'I believe him when he says he only been suffering for the last six months.'

'I see. That is most helpful to know.'

William added, 'I believe Mr Atkins is a very reliable witness, although of course I would wager it is always possible that he may have failed to tell me everything.'

'Yes,' Hunter agreed, 'in my experience they seldom do that which is why it is vital to interrogate the patient more than just once, unless of course the malady is simple or obvious.'

'Indeed, that is very true and wise,' said William.

The surgeon continued to clarify several additional points about Mr Atkins.

'You mention in your letter that he had suffered from venereal disease during his long service in the navy. Can you tell me a trifle more about that?'

'Yes I can,' answered William, 'so far as I had gleaned from his testimony Mr Atkins suffered from both the pox…'

'You mean syphilis?'

'Yes indeed syphilis and he also had at least one attack of gonorrhoea. Of this I am certain.'

'Good. And do you know what treatment, if any, your patient received for these distressing ailments?'

'I am sorry I do not know the details but I believe he had some treatment to ease his symptoms, presumably some poultices and soothing ointments.'

'That is important to know and I suggest you interview Mr Atkins again and determine if you can, exactly what treatment he had for these maladies which are so very common in sailors.'

William concurred. 'Yes I shall certainly do that. I also believe that syphilis and gonorrhoea have the same cause, presumably some kind of germ.'

'Yes I believe that to be the case, especially as they tend to occur together. But we do not know that for certain and I predict that their true causes will only become clearer with time and more work. We need more scientific investigation of human diseases.'

'Indeed sir, and you are a pioneer of that noble branch of knowledge.'

''I thank you sir for that. I do my best but there is always so much for we doctors and scientists to learn.'

'That is certainly the case,' agreed William.

Hunter went on. 'There are more concerns here. You said he once worked as a hatter. Do you know the duration of that employment and whether he had a specialty?'

'I am afraid I do not know for certain the duration though I believe it was for a few years. I do know that he was very proficient at making felt hats.'

'I see. How interesting.'

At this point Hunter sat down, thought for a few seconds, and wrote down a few notes on a large piece of paper using one of the many quilt pens lying on the top of his large mahogany desk.

'Is there anything else that I should be doing Mr Hunter?'

'Yes, there is. I am concerned about this sect, or whatever it is, that Mr Atkins has joined. I have a fear that these people, whoever they are, may be a malign influence on your patient. There are some very peculiar and bad coves lurking throughout London and only too eager to take advantage of those who are gullible, weak or infirm. I suggest if you possibly can that you try to meet with some of these people and assess the types of people they are. I am sure they are not actually poisoning him but it is prudent to keep every possibility in mind. All this may not answer but I think it should be done.'

'I shall certainly do that,' said William.

'Good. I hope my comments have been helpful. I have ventured to give you considerably more work to do.'

'You have been extremely helpful sir. I shall see to all these points directly.'

'Good. Please arrange to see me again for further consultation when you have finished.'

'I shall certainly do that,' agreed William.

John Hunter then seemed to relax and became less serious and more congenial.

'I also wanted to make you aware, if you were not already so, that my colleague Mr John Aubrey has recently had yet another success with his lithotomy operation.'

'Do you mean the one performed on Sir Joshua Turner just this last month?'

'Yes that is the very one. Oh, I do believe you yourself were present at the operation…'

'Yes I was present. It was all over within three minutes at most.'

'Well that is still not as fast as one of my old teachers Mr William Cheselden, who as you may know passed away sixteen years ago. Three minutes is fast to be sure, but Cheselden was lightning fast and managed to perform this procedure in a remarkable one minute. But no matter, Sir Joshua recovered from the procedure very well and is already working again.'

'You mean he is already making a great deal of money again?'

'Yes, quite so. You are certainly in the right about that.'

This seemed a good moment for William to take his leave. Accordingly, he thanked the great surgeon for his time and advice, bowed, and left him free to get on with his writing and scientific research.

*

Rather to William's surprise, there was no difficulty in arranging an early meeting with two prominent members of the sect or group that seemed to be so influential in Abraham Atkin's life. Whether this was because they were genuinely open to his scrutiny, or whether this apparent openness was more of a ruse to mislead him, he remained unsure. But, together with a strong sense of unease, he was determined to find out as much as he could about them while intent on revealing as little as possible about himself, his medical brethren and their suspicions. When they heard about the location of his own home, it was agreed by all three of them to meet up in 'The Old Burlington' which was a popular public house which could be found along Church Street in Chiswick, a most convenient venue that was just a few hundred yards' walking distance from William's residence.

*

Around three o'clock in the afternoon, on a Friday just one week after his most helpful meeting with John Hunter, William found himself waiting for his two 'guests' in the historic public house in Chiswick. He was sitting on an uncomfortable wooden stool with both his elbows resting on the plain round wooden table placed in front of him. The room in which he was sitting was situated in the front of the atmospheric building, and about twenty feet to his left there was a small door which led to the large taproom where he could see a cluster of men holding pewter tankards of ale and engaged in what seemed like convivial banter. All around him were low wooden tables around which many men, most middle-aged but also some who were rather younger, seemed immersed in either business transactions of some kind or else just harmless gossip. William also saw one or two women sitting among them, most of whom were sipping from small wine glasses, but who remained quiet on the whole. His vision of this generally happy and relaxed scene was somewhat obscured by thick clouds of tobacco smoke which emanated in various circular and more complex patterns from several of these regular patrons who were quietly smoking their clay pipes. The entire premises had a reassuringly homely smell consisting of beer, wood and tobacco smoke.

Being of a courteous nature, he had not yet ordered any liquid refreshment as he wished to wait until the others had arrived.

*

He did not have to wait long. Just five minutes after the appointed time he saw two people enter the main door of the pub, a young man probably in his early thirties and a younger woman whom he thought was most likely in her late twenties. Both had a rather nervous but very alert expression, and after their gaze was directed towards him they immediately smiled in recognition and walked briskly towards his table. It certainly seemed to him like recognition at first sight which he found slightly surprising. The man was very tall and lean with a sallow complexion, and was wearing a dull grey frock coat, a plain blue waistcoat without any embroidery and light brown breeches. The younger woman was also much taller than average - in fact about the same height as William - and had clear, quite striking, facial features which suggested both determination and intelligence. She wore a long light blue robe without any embellishments and wore her hair quite high with a neat garland of flowers at the top which seemed to hold it in place. His immediate assessment was that they were not particularly well dressed and yet were neither members of an elite professional class nor poor. Either that or they had deliberately donned these particular clothes to convey a particularly neutral impression. But for all he knew these might also be their best clothes. The man removed his brown tricorn hat as he approached William's table and introduced himself.

'You must be the distinguished Dr Aston sir.'

As he said this he made a deep leg to show his respect. William immediately rose from his table and bowed, but not quite so low, to convey his own respect.

'Yes I am the same. I am William Aston, at your

service sir,' and then looking at the woman, 'Madam at your service.'

'James Arkwright, your servant sir, and I have the honour to present Miss Elizabeth Ansted.' At this the woman gave a polite curtsey and smiled at him. William then bowed again.

'It is a pleasure to meet you both,' said William, 'and thank you so much for coming to speak with me.'

'We are delighted to converse with you about our good friend Abraham,' started James, 'we were truly distressed to learn of his recent infirmity. We do so hope he may yet recover.'

'Well,' William replied, 'we truly do not know what the future holds for the poor man. But we medical men are all agreed that he is a sick man. The main question is what is ailing him.' At this both James and Elizabeth looked just a little more anxious than William might have expected. But perhaps they were just very concerned for their friend.

'So what exactly do you think is the matter with him?' asked Elizabeth.

'The truth of it is that we don't know, but he seems to have a failing of part of his nervous system,' replied William.

'You mean he is more nervous than he should be by rights?' asked James.

William smiled benignly at this complete misunderstanding.

'No I mean the nerves in his body that control his arms and legs and also such faculties as his memory and general state of mind.'

'Oh I understand. It signifies something completely different then?' said James.

'It does,' replied William.

There was then an uncomfortable silence of about fifteen seconds.

But William was keen to broach the subject in hand as soon as possible.

'But we must take some refreshment. What may I get for you fine people?' he asked.

'Thank you kindly sir. I shall have a tankard of beer if you please,' replied James.

'And I shall have a small glass of sherry sir if that is acceptable to you,' said Elizabeth.

'And I shall also have a beer to join you sir,' said William.

He gestured discreetly to an overworked waitress

who was standing with arms akimbo nearby and politely ordered their drinks.

He used the time they had to wait for them to address the main issue more directly. 'So may I ask you how you first met Mr Atkins?'

'Yes of course,' replied James, 'but the way of it was that Abraham came to us rather than the other way round. He had heard about our organisation you will understand and was most keen to join us.'

'May I ask what type of organisation yours is?' William was already sceptical in his mind.

'We are a mixture of about twenty like-minded folk, and all very respectably employed in various ways I might add, who have formed a small group of brethren.'

'You mean you are Christians?' asked William.

'No,' replied James, 'none of us are religious in the common way of things though I am sure all of us are God-fearing in some form or other. What I mean is that we have formed a brotherhood and sisterhood which aims to do good to people who have fallen by the wayside or who are suffering greatly from poverty or lack of an honest day's work.'

'I see, I think,' said William, who was not seeing at

all though for certain he was thinking. 'So if I understand you correctly, you are rather like Quaker folk who believe profoundly in peace and goodwill to all men and women, though you do not profess to be Christians.'

'Well that is not entirely correct, and we are very different from Quakers, but in these other peaceful aspects you are probably in the right of it.'

'Good. I see. So Abraham heard about your organisation, or brethren, and knew that you might be able to assist him in some way.'

'Yes he was very much down on his luck and had only occasional employment.'

'As a porter in Billingsgate market you mean.'

'Yes that is precisely so, but we are not able to provide coin for such people much as they might most assuredly desire it. What we can offer is congenial friendship and support in the hope that we can provide some welcome spiritual enrichment for their souls.'

'I think I understand what you are about,' said William. He was beginning to worry.

'That is very good,' added Elizabeth who was now focussing her gaze on William's face as the three drinks were brought to the table by the waitress who smiled as she did so.

William took a few sips from his tankard and continued his gentle questioning.

'Will you please give me leave to ask you both how you found Abraham's behaviour and general stability of mind these last few months when you saw him at your meetings?'

James immediately replied without any hesitation, almost as if this was a question he had expected to be asked.

'I am glad you have questioned me on that. To be candid, we all found that Abraham was a little excitable at first, perhaps just a few months ago, but after that he often appeared to be very out of sorts and sometimes showed us all his hot temper. We were all quite alarmed…'

'Quite shocked at the change in him,' interjected Elizabeth.

'Yes I can well believe that,' said William, 'so did you decide to do anything about this irksome change in his usually gentle nature?'

'Not at first,' replied James.

'Not at first?'

'Indeed, at first we thought it was just a sudden trifle, or a loss of his usual sanguine demeanour. But then it all became much worse after about two months and we advised him and also his sister that he should seek the advice of a medical person as soon as possible.'

'But that would be quite expensive would it not?' asked William.

'Yes but needs must, yet he was most unwilling to seek help.'

'So what did you do?' At last William felt he was getting somewhere with these two rather evasive individuals.

'We wanted to help him so we gave him a tonic that we had obtained from one of our brethren, who was fortunately an apothecary by trade.'

'I see,' said William, 'and do you know what this tonic contained exactly?'

James looked slightly uneasy just for a second but William saw the man's expression change nevertheless.

'Oh it was all harmless stuff, just some coloured water and a few additional ingredients. I do believe, so the apothecary told us, that there was also a minute amount of laudanum contained within the tonic, only to help his agitated state of mind you understand.'

'Yes I do see,' replied William, 'laudanum is not exactly what I would describe as a harmless medicine but I doubt it would have done him any harm if it was such a miniscule dose,' James continued.

'Anyway it didn't make a ha'penny's worth of difference to his mood which only became more agitated and we never gave him any more of the tonic.'

'I understand. And then he somehow came to the attention of Mr Aubrey at St George's hospital and thence to myself, as we all know very well.'

'Yes that is entirely correct, and there was nothing more we could do for him.'

'Actually,' added Elizabeth, 'he was getting so destructive and angry that we were seriously disposed to asking him to cease attending our meetings.'

'But that was not necessary in the end,' said James, 'since about a month before he saw Mr Aubrey he stopped attending our weekly meetings anyway .'

'So none of you has set eyes on Abraham for about the last six weeks,' stated William, 'is that correct?'

'Yes absolutely,' they both replied in strange unison.

'Well sir, madam, you have both been most helpful

and I am most grateful to you for your time.'

'We are delighted to have been of some use to you, sir. We just hope so very much that you will be able to do something for poor Abraham. We feel so badly for the poor soul.'

'Well,' said William wistfully, 'we will do our best, but it is probably in God's hands from now on rather than our own.'

At this James and Elizabeth looked at each other quizzically but said nothing.

After this was said, all three got up, left the building and made their own way to whatever destination was appropriate for them. In William's case it was his own home. But as he walked back to the pleasures of domestic bliss he felt very uneasy about the conversation with these two people. Alarm bells were certainly ringing but they may still have been irrelevant to his patient's illness, whatever that was. He reckoned only time would tell.

CHAPTER 9

A diagnosis is established

Just two weeks after their first meeting, in which they had discussed the difficult case of Henry McNeil Grayson, a very excited Rupert Aston phoned his neurological colleague John Rapello to tell him about the latest investigation results.

'John,' he said down the telephone sitting on his office desk, 'I think we have a diagnosis on Mr Grayson. It was all because of your insight. Can you come round to my office right now? I want to show you something.'

'Yes of course Rupert. How exciting. Give me five minutes,' was the reply.

Ten minutes later the two doctors were sitting in Rupert's small, book-lined and rather untidy office in the outpatient department. John's eager manner was matched only by Rupert's obvious excitement. Rupert was unsure as to whether he should present the test results in a logical sequence or else just cut to the chase, so to speak, and give the key test result immediately. In the end his sense of drama favoured the first option.

'Right,' Rupert began, 'let's start with the additional tests you had suggested.'

'Fair enough, sure.'

'OK, so we repeated the MRI of the brain with those special FLAIR sequences you advised. The result was the same and there was no thalamic pulvinar enhancement.'

'So it was normal.'

'Yes it was completely normal. Then we re-examined the CSF which was again normal and we did not detect the 14-3-3 protein.'

'Right, that's good,' said John.

'We also repeated the electrodiagnostic studies and the report came back saying that it was again completely normal with no evidence of either a peripheral neuropathy or lower motor neuron problem.'

'Fair enough, so it's not CJD. How about the

neuropsychology assessment?'

'Yes I was coming to that. It certainly showed a marked deterioration in his intellectual function. His full scale IQ was 102 whereas the estimated premorbid IQ was on the high side as at least 125, assuming you believe all that stuff. He also had marked impairment of short-term memory and as well as some formal tests of comprehension and understanding. These abnormalities are definitely not functional.'

'So,' John interjected 'there was unequivocal evidence that his mental functioning was significantly impaired in an organic way.'

'Yes, that was definite. No question about it and that also has to be interpreted in relation to his emotional lability, and the fact that just about everyone who knows him thinks he is going slowly crazy.'

'So there is no question about that.'

'No, there isn't. But we then come to his associates, two of whom I met.'

'Ah,' John said, 'the dreaded sect.'

'Well actually I'm not sure what they should be called. After my meeting with two of their key members I was almost certain they were a pretty harmless lot, and also, by the way, they weren't particularly religious and I wouldn't call them a sect. My overall impression is that they were a bunch of self-appointed do-gooders, a bit cracked maybe, but essentially harmless. And for sure they weren't trying to poison him.'

'Right so that rules out what we always thought was a very unlikely possibility.'

'It does indeed.'

'So now,' John said in an uncharacteristic quiet tone, 'no doubt you are going to hit me with a surprise result.'

Rupert smiled and showed him a single sheet of paper, a pathology report.

'Well John you suggested a toxicology screen and I'm so glad you did because frankly I'm sure I would have missed it otherwise.'

John put on his reading glasses and examined the report intensely. Rupert continued.

'All the routine blood tests, including the examination of blood smears, renal and liver function, glucose, autoantibodies, vitamin B12 and all that came back normal. A random urine sample was normal but then in view of what you had said about poisoning and heavy metals and that kind of stuff, I decided to do a 24-hour urinary collection and analyse that.'

'So you then found something?' asked John clearly now on tenterhooks.

'Yes... wait for it. His urinary mercury level was way above the normal range, in fact it was at the ceiling!'

John looked upwards as if to pray to heaven and then clapped his hands together.

'Of course that's the answer,' he exclaimed, 'it explains everything. Why is everything so obvious in retrospect?'

'Maybe because one then feels one should have got the diagnosis earlier.'

'Perhaps you're right about that, but anyway we got there in the end.'

'I think John that "we" is the operative word there. You know I could not have got there without your help.'

'I think you would have actually, though maybe it would have taken a little while longer. By the way, you can confirm a diagnosis of mercury poisoning by examining the hair, especially if it is chronic rather than acute. He does have some hair I hope.'

'He does and I have already done that. I don't have

the official report yet but I just phoned the toxicology lab this morning and the guy there told me that the mercury level in the hair sample we sent them was extremely high.'

'So that's terrific. We have game, set and match then.'

Rupert smiled before answering.

'Well yes and no. We have a diagnosis but we are not completely sure why his mercury level is so high and also my understanding is that chronic mercury poisoning is not so easy to treat as is acute poisoning. So he may still die.'

'Yes he could die of it for sure. But what's the cause?'

'Well,' Rupert continued, 'there are clues in the detailed history and I am pretty sure he has at least two environmental risk factors. I've been reading up a little about this and surprisingly eating fish contaminated with mercury is probably the commonest cause of inadvertent ingestion of mercury. When later I delved into his diet in more detail if I found out to my amazement that Henry, though not in any way wealthy, had been eating large amounts of tuna fish at least four times a week for over ten years.'

'Wow that is a lot of tuna fish. But how did he afford it?'

'I don't know how, but he did. He told me so and I believe him. Why should he lie?'

John nodded in agreement.

'Rupert, I guess that is enough to explain things. But isn't there another factor in the history?'

'I know, I know, you mean the gold mining period in West Africa.'

'Yes precisely, I know he only worked there for about two years, but poor or inadequate processing of gold extraction during that time may have been enough to raise his body's level of mercury to above or just above normal, and that could well have been significant and predisposed him to further mercury contamination.'

Rupert thought for a few seconds and then shrugged.

'Yes that's perfectly credible, but the key thing I suppose is that we have a secure diagnosis which I am sure can explain the whole clinical picture so it just can't be a red herring. Also, thank goodness, we now know that he wasn't deliberately poisoned. You know I was really dreading that possibility.'

John agreed.

'Yes I don't think we need investigate him any further. But I am not sure how bright the future is for him.'

'That's difficult to predict for sure. I wouldn't like to be in his shoes.'

'They wouldn't fit you!' John retorted, giving a small version of his signature machine gun laugh.

'That's also true.'

'So how will you treat him, assuming you can of course.'

'Well,' Rupert replied, 'I need to get more advice from the toxicologists and the metabolic people, but from what I have read some form of chelation therapy like dimercaprol, may be the best first option but I doubt we will be able to do anything more than just slow or perhaps even halt the degenerative process. But you never know, he might still surprise us.'

'Well,' John added, 'for sure he certainly surprised me!'

CHAPTER 10

No diagnosis is established

William sat motionless at his wooden study desk and sighed deeply. He felt that he was already making real progress in discovering the true cause or causes of Abraham Atkin's progressive malady, and he had derived great benefit from the wise advice given to him so generously by Mr John Hunter. But then providence struck. It was a particularly cruel blow especially for the patient, but also for him and indeed the entire profession of medical practice. Just three weeks after he had first set eyes on Abraham, the poor man had suddenly collapsed with what looked like a serious fit of apoplexy and rapidly expired the following day. Naturally William felt deeply sorry for Abraham, and also his devoted sister whom he imagined would have been devastated by her loss, but at the same time he was very distressed that he had not had more time to make enquiries and gain more understanding of the gentleman's curious and most troublesome illness. Mr Atkins's physical and mental suffering had ended for certain, but now only God alone would know what truly ailed him.

*

It was eight o'clock in the evening, and the air in the room was comfortably warm. William always found the summer months in London so much more agreeable than those in winter despite the appalling smells and stale air that was disposed to pollute many of the narrower streets during a typical London summer. Yet despite such trials and drawbacks, he still preferred the comfort of a barmy June evening to the chilblains, hacks and biting winds that so often characterise the chilly months of December to March. Christmas may offer some relief and temporary enjoyment during this time but such seasonal festivities did not manage to assuage either his or Lizzie's prolonged physical torment. Perhaps if they were not so lean then they might suffer less but he rather doubted that. As he contemplated both the tragedy of Abraham Atkins and the pain of winter he could hear with great clarity the reassuring sounds of his wife playing Bach on their spinet in the drawing room below him. Listening to those perfectly balanced notes and counterpoints provided him with some comfort, especially since they were played so well and symmetrically by his beloved wife, but it was the genius of the composer who must take the credit for the mental joy that the musical treasure somehow managed to produce on every single occasion. It was always a surprise to him that Bach was so generally under-appreciated, but that, just like everything else in this life, might alter in due course. Fashions change - he had already witnessed that phenomenon during his own life regarding such trifles as clothes, wigs and manners - but certain other aspects of life remained eternal, and they must have been created by our Lord.

Try as he might, he could not get the vision of those two members of the sect, brethren, company or whatever they might call themselves, out of his thoughts. They may have been harmless, and done Abraham no ill, but all the same he most certainly did not like them. He was more than a trifle suspicious of their motives in assisting him but he was unable to be sure of their true intentions. He found them both somewhat evasive in their answers to his questions, and he was also observant and sufficiently subtle to notice the clandestine looks they gave each other at several moments during their conversation with him. William was particularly perplexed by the so-called 'tonic' they had decided to give him. What did that liquid truly consist of? They said there was a minute amount of laudanum in it that was included to calm his increasingly nervous disposition and hot temper, but he was not sure whether that was the whole truth. Were there other far less benign components in that tonic and would a tiny dose of laudanum truly calm his excitable demeanour? He rather suspected the first of these conjectures was true and the second was probably false. But now it was just too late for either he or his medical and surgical colleagues to ascertain the truth of the matter. Mr Aubrey was most sanguine and relaxed when he informed him of Abraham's sudden demise and indeed was just a touch philosophical about it.

'Do not upset yourself William,' the eminent surgeon had said, trying to console him, 'people die all the time and besides you did your very best and I am most terribly grateful to you for all your concern and advice.'

The surgeon's kindness certainly helped him to an extent but it did not entirely remove the anguish and developing sense of failure that he could not help but feel.

William had not yet told Mr John Hunter officially

about the sudden death of his patient though word of mouth in the hospital had probably already reached him. He suspected that the great man would want to have a post-mortem examination if at all possible but permission for that would be very unlikely to be given. Also, there were insufficient suspicious features surrounding his death to justify a coroner's inquest, and besides the entire region of Westminster only allows about fifty of these per year so this was a rarity in London. He never managed to have a further discussion with Mr Hunter after all the additional enquiries about Mr Atkins's case had been made. Indeed, as God was his witness there was absolutely nothing he could do. However he did decide to write the case up in detail. His purpose was to document the case for posterity. Thus he wrote a detailed pamphlet entitled as follows:

JOURNAL OF DR WILLIAM ASTON, PRACTISING PHYSICIAN OF LONDON DURING THE YEAR OF OUR LORD 1768 INCLUDING SOME REMARKS CONCERNING A MOST INTERESTING PATIENT.

CHAPTER 11

History may or may not repeat itself

Rupert closed the historic journal after he had read the final page. He was appalled and fascinated in equal measure, but he was also very perplexed, and experienced a curious surge of almost vicarious frustration. After all, this man, Abraham Atkins, had died two hundred and fifty years previously. Quite apart from the remarkable, if not somewhat voyeuristic, privilege of reading someone else's journal, he saw an extraordinary similarity between the illnesses of Abraham Atkins and Henry Grayson. But clearly his distant medical ancestor William Aston deliberately wrote this journal to enable people to read it and make their own judgement in the light of much hoped for medical advances in the future. So he should not feel any sense of unease. While he already knew about the relatively primitive state of medicine and surgery in the eighteenth century, nevertheless he was still pretty shocked at this contemporary testimony so clearly laid out in the journal. Furthermore, he could not fail to perceive what he thought was a certain similarity between the characters of William and himself. He found that quite destabilising, but he had never read anything in either current or historical textbooks or popular journals about Dr William Aston that would suggest that he had made any major contributions to medicine during his lifetime. His ancestral records told him that William had lived to the age of eighty-three years until 1813 which for that period was a very long life. Actually that wasn't a bad innings for anyone in the twenty-first century. But Rupert was certain that his medical ancestor had been a successful and generally well respected, if not hugely wealthy or eminent, physician during his lifetime.

*

As he leaned back in his office swivel chair and clasped his hands behind his head, Rupert tried hard to think logically about the similarities between the two cases. He found himself doing this automatically so perhaps he was in a sense being deliberately manipulated by a voice from the past. Be that as it may, and in truth he rather doubted that anyway, he straightened back up, picked up a blue biro pen from his desk and started to make notes on a blank sheet of A4 paper that was conveniently lying on his large wooden desk.

*

First, he thought about his own patient Henry McNeil Grayson, who had already shown possible signs of slight improvement with the chelation treatment recommended by his toxicology colleagues. Thank goodness, he told himself, for the wonders and advances of modern medicine. He literally shuddered at the thought of suffering from certain conditions had he lived in the eighteenth century. He and his helpful colleagues had determined unequivocally that Henry had suffered from chronic mercury poisoning the cause or causes of which were completely inadvertent and which had mainly attacked his nervous system. He had just been very unlucky in his employment and eating habits. The diagnosis had been established as a result of both clinical acumen and technological advances in the laboratory, and not without a little assistance from his colleagues. But what was the true diagnosis in his ancestor's patient, the hapless Abraham Atkins? What did he *really* die of? In terms of the final illness that suddenly killed him, Rupert suspected that was something acute like a massive heart attack, or maybe even a major stroke or a large pulmonary embolism. These possible disasters, fatal and terrible as they were, could not, however, have been the cause of his chronic illness lasting almost a year and which, from what he had gleaned from William's journal, had also attacked the nervous system producing limb weakness, tremor and an array of neuro-behavioural symptoms. No, they were caused by something else. But what was it?

*

The clues were all written in the journal for anyone who was alert to their presence. Rupert also suspected that had Abraham lived longer than the brilliant John Hunter would have managed to get to the bottom of things. First, Abraham had worked as a hatter before he joined the navy. It had long been established that making hats, in particular felt hats which was Abraham's special skill, exposed the hatters to the dangers of inorganic mercury. That is why some people in the past used the phrase 'mad as a hatter' including the author Lewis Carroll in *Alice in Wonderland*. That could well have been a factor in his illness despite the long interval between exposure and the apparent development of symptoms. He guessed that John Hunter had picked up this point though he had said nothing at the time. Next, Abraham had been in the Royal Navy for many years and it certainly sounded as if he had suffered from a bout of scurvy while on Commodore Anson's circumnavigation of the seas, an affliction that was later recognised to be treatable with fresh fruit though the role of vitamins, vitamin C in this case, was only discovered later in the beginning of the twentieth century. He had, like so many sailors during that period, also suffered from venereal disease. Assuming he had syphilis, which was more than likely, the ship's surgeon, or other available medical person, would doubtless have treated him with mercury which had been regarded as an effective cure for 'the pox' at the time and also for many years after that. Such barbaric treatment was the basis for the popular phrase 'A night with Venus means a lifetime with Mercury'. That was most unfortunate but in many instances perfectly true at the time. So those two factors could certainly explain his neurological features and behaviour disturbance on the basis of chronic mercury poisoning.

*

But that may not be the end of the case. There were still some gaps and anomalies that no-one might ever understand. Why did William make such a point about his suspicion and clear dislike of those two members of the sect or group which had befriended

Abraham? What was their true purpose in doing so? Rupert supposes, as had his ancestor, that the so-called 'tonic' they had given him might in reality have contained a poison, and for all he knows that could have been mercury. Perhaps, having first ensnared him into their group in the hope that he could have been a useful contact or ally, they later feared him as he became increasingly unhinged due to his underlying illness. So they reckoned he was a threat and decided literally to expel him using a slow poison which may or may not have contained mercury. While that was a perfectly feasible possibility, it did sound very far-fetched to Rupert. Maybe they were just innocent cranks. That thought made him shiver slightly when he suddenly saw the similarity between that rather sinister group and the bunch of misguided do-gooders who had befriended his own patient Mr Grayson.

*

Then he supposed there was always the possibility of a dietary cause of mercury poisoning. While this had definitely been the key issue in Mr Grayson's case, he was far less sure in the case of his ancestor. Abraham had been a seaman in the Royal Navy for well over a decade and may have developed a taste for seafood including tuna, shark and whale. If so, then that could have led to excessive consumption of fish contaminated with mercury. He had also worked as a porter in Billingsgate fish market where he would also have had access to contaminated fish which may have caused him to ingest mercury inadvertently. But these two possibilities, while intriguing, were in truth just speculation, and certainly no more than that. The first two factors were far more credible explanations of Abraham's condition.

*

It was getting late in the evening, half past ten to be exact, and Rupert was tired from the day's hard work at the hospital. His eyes were also beginning to ache and water from the effort required in deciphering the deceptively neat handwriting of William's journal. He was almost completely certain that he had worked out the apparent mystery of his medical ancestor's patient and just wished that he had just one or two hair samples from the past that he could give to his toxicology colleagues for their expert analysis. But of course William Aston, though clearly both moral and very conscientious, did not have the gift of prophesy.

*

Nine months later, while Rupert was busy speaking into his dictating machine after finishing his weekly new outpatient clinic, he flipped the stop switch, sat back in his uncomfortable wooden chair and started to think about Henry Grayson. Having established unequivocally a diagnosis of chronic mercury poisoning, a diagnostic feat that had clearly impressed many of his hospital colleagues thereby enhancing his already fine reputation as a sharp diagnostician, he was more than gratified that his patient had done well after chelation therapy and had stopped deteriorating altogether. Indeed, some people, including his family doctor, had actually thought he'd improved somewhat, but even the optimistic Rupert didn't think that was very likely. But it was certainly possible he supposed. One never can tell with these things.

*

Soon afterwards he strode down the long corridor at his usual fast pace to his own personal office, still small but slightly larger than the tiny consulting room where had just seen his six new patients for the morning, and started to eat a frugal lunch of a tuna sandwich and low fat fruit yoghurt, all washed down with a strong mug of filtered coffee from the machine perched somewhat precariously on the far window sill. He made the bitter coffee more drinkable by adding a touch of milk from the small fridge in the room. Just after he had finished eating, which he did in no more than five minutes, he sifted through the morning's mail. He threw most of it straight into the waste bin as it was advertising rubbish, but one letter addressed to him personally in neat handwriting caught his attention. He carefully opened the envelope with his right thumb, removed the two page handwritten letter it contained and slowly read its contents with increasing astonishment and no small degree of alarm.

Dear Dr Aston.

I hope you don't mind my writing to you directly. I am still so incredibly grateful to you for sorting out my illness. I am as you know not due to see you again for another two months at the hospital. You will be very pleased I'm sure to know that I am keeping quite well and have definitely not got any worse and I may even have improved a bit. My arm tremors are now less of a problem and I feel much better in myself and feel much less anxious. In fact, believe it or not, I just got employed full-time as a porter at the Royal Naval Hospital in Greenwich. I think they must have been influenced by the fact that I had spent fifteen years in the Merchant Navy as a seaman! What a sympathetic lot! Anyway I am now employed.

Now for the shock news, which I could hardly believe. I got very interested in family trees, geneology and all that stuff. This was mainly due to my younger brother Jack who contacted me a few months ago after a quiet interval of almost eight years when I never even saw him. He had been looking into our ancestry - he got some company or other to look into it. He has always been obsessed by such things in our family past. It was incredible as he managed to go back about ten generations as far as the 1700s would you believe! Anyway, around the middle of the eighteenth century there was a ten time grandfather of ours called Abraham Atkins who apparently had sailed with George Anson in 1740. Incredible, so I am not the first sailor in my family! This man died in 1768 aged forty–eight years and as far as Jack could make out he had suffered from symptoms that were very similar to the ones I have. He had 'the shakes', was progressively 'weak limbed' and suffered from a 'surfeit of anxiety and unpredictable behaviour.' I just wondered whether he had been suffering from a similar disease to my own. I am sure this is just a coincidence, but it still shook me to the core when I heard about it. Needless to say, my brother Jack didn't think anything of it. I must add that I don't know of any hereditary diseases in our family.

Anyway I just wanted to let you know about this because I think it is so very interesting, and I hope you find it interesting too.

I look forward to seeing you again at the hospital in two months.

Yours truly

Henry Grayson.

PS. I almost forgot to mention that I recently stopped smoking. I am a reformed character!

Rupert put down the letter onto his desk and sat down. In doing so he almost slipped off his chair and fell to the floor as he was in a state of shock. He had difficulty in believing what he had just read but it was all written down clearly in black and white. He certainly needed to speak to this Jack character to find out more about what he had uncovered in their family tree, but there was still no getting away from the facts. What he really needed was time to think about all this and what it might mean.

*

The truth of it, or so it seemed to Rupert, was that there were only two possible explanations of what he had just been told. There was no equivocation, no middle way, and no third reason. Yes, for sure it was definitely extraordinary but he had to think rationally. Either this was a complete coincidence or it was not. That was it. His logical self was telling him that it was merely a remarkable coincidence and that he should not think any more of it. But that was not his instinctive gut feeling, the one that was invariably correct in his medical practice. The other explanation was surreal, and was that these two men were somehow linked in time and had both suffered from the same disease which was chronic mercury poisoning. He knows that no-one else could possibly have read William Aston's personal journal as he had the only known copy. The similarities were simply too close for them to be merely coincidental, in particular the possible influence of a rather sinister group of apparently benign though misguided do-gooders. No, there was too much that was in complete synch here. He could just about understand a kind of medical-type link between William Aston in the mid-eighteenth century and himself in the twenty-first century. But to have a simultaneous link between distant relatives both suffering from the same disease was just out of the question. It was too much of an imaginative stretch to be credible naturally.

It was only when he thought further about the implications of this second instinctive explanation that Rupert became more agitated and frightened. If this were really true, then so many other things might also be true. The supernatural might be a reality, ghosts may exist, a sixth sense may exist, clairvoyance might exist, other inhabited worlds might exist - in fact just about every supernatural event the existence of which all rational people have always questioned might very well exist. If even some of those events and beliefs were actually true, then his entire world view must be based on unreality. What he had always thought of as real might not be real at all.

Whatever the truth of the matter might be, his perception of the world in which he lived had changed forever.

How was he expected to live with such a notion?

ABOUT THE AUTHOR

Peter Kennedy CBE, MD, PhD, DSc is a distinguished clinician and scientist who held the Burton Chair of Neurology for 29 years (1987-2016) at the University of Glasgow where he remains active in research and teaching as an Honorary Senior Research Fellow in the Institute of Infection, Immunity and Inflammation. He also has two Masters degrees in Philosophy, and has written five previous novels, an award winning popular science book on African Sleeping sickness, and co-edited two textbooks on neurological infections. He is a fellow of both the Royal Society of Edinburgh and the Academy of Medical Sciences.

PETER KENNEDY

BY THE SAME AUTHOR
ALSO AVAILABLE ON AMAZON:

THE IMAGE IN MY MIND (2020)
ARCADIAN MEMORIES AND OTHER POEMS (2020)
THE FATAL SLEEP (2019) - Luath Press, 3rd Edition
TWELVE MONTHS OF FREEDOM (2019)
CATAPULT IN TIME (2018)
RETURN OF THE CIRCLE (2017)
BROTHERS IN RETRIBUTION (2015)
REVERSAL OF DAVID (2014).

Printed in Great Britain
by Amazon